BEFORE THE BLOOD
JOHN SIMONS

By Denise M. Baran-Unland

Cover art by Sue Midlock

Frontispiece by Christopher Gleason

PRINTED IN THE UNITED STATES OF AMERICA

This book is a work of fiction. Names, characters, businesses, organizations, places, events, and incidents are the product of the author's imagination. Any resemblance is purely coincidental.

Cover art by Sue Midlock
Frontispiece by Christopher Gleason

ISBN 978-1-949777-01-7
www.bryonyseries.com

This book is lovingly dedicated to the reader, whoever you might be.

He had vowed to play or die; he just might get the latter.

THE PROLOGUE

"Hurry, sir! Oh please, hurry!"

He paused again, and then reluctantly shut the accounts book. The third floor on the east wing was the last place he intended to step, but he supposed he must, if only to silence her persistent grating cry. So, the infant could die? So the *mother* could die? Well, what was that to him?

During his years on the streets, hawking anything he could steal, he'd seen plenty of death: six-year-olds frozen to death between buildings, old men's throats slit over half loaves of bread, drunken brawls ending with gunshots and blood splattered across the doorway of his hidey hole. His lungs had weathered the thick dust and cotton lint of the textile mill; his cunning had made him the man he was today: whole, sound, successful.

What irony Adrianna's death had broken him!

The housemaid scuttled through the hall, but he walked with even, deliberate steps. Adrianna had lived two hours, not long enough to see the sunrise of her birthday, just long enough to open her pale blue eyes and gaze into his paler ones as he willed each feeble breath, breaths growing fainter, farther apart, and more elusive as the minutes ticked away. Still cradled in his arms, Adrianna gasped her last in the hour before dawn.

Despite these consequences, *she* had lured him into to her rooms anyway, and for what? *For this?* He should've been stronger. He should've retained a mistress sooner. Here was the sad result.

They entered the birthing chamber, and he recoiled against the stifling stench of sweat, human waste, and blood.

Why was it always blood?

The midwife offered him a bundle. Hands clenched behind him, he glanced at it with contempt. The squawking creature wrapped in a snow-white blanket, embellished with many hours of his wife's patient, careful, hopeful-of-the-future needlework, lacked any of Adrianna's beauty or grace. This one resembled a skinned opossum.

His wife lay at the other end of the room, propped on mountains of the finest down. Her chalky face sank between masses of abundant hair, the hair he once luxuriated in brushing to gleaming gold while reveling in its weight between his hands and burying his nose in its scent. He gagged at the memory. She held out a thin, weak hand. Repulsed, he stepped back.

"He's perfect," she said.

He shuddered at her openness. Couldn't she see he no longer wanted her, that her very image filled him with deep revulsion?

She continued gazing at him with begging eyes. "Abbott, we can still raise the family we planned. I've named him...."

"Label him what you will," he answered indifferently. "Anything but my name."

He glared at the midwife on the way out the door.

"You needn't have tried so hard to save him." Abbott looked back. "He'll never amount to much."

CHAPTER ONE: ONE MAGICAL CHRISTMAS

The man in the long frock coat and extra-wide cravat had stared at her with peculiar steadiness all night, almost as if goading her to notice him. His defiant confidence intrigued her and caused those sneaky peeks to see if he was still watching.

Earlier in the day, Lucetta had caught a glimpse of his all-consuming gaze when she was setting the table for tonight's party. In that moment, she was not the recipient of the gaze; rather, he had beheld something in his hand with an expression of studious disbelief.

Christine, peering into the room, had squealed under her breath, "Oooh, what an ugly man!"

Lucetta couldn't help agreeing with her baby sister, but the man, barely five feet tall, hair swept off his forehead, gray-blond strands brushing his high collar, and a severe look to his unlined face although he was obviously past forty, also had a demeanor about him that made her want to know him, even though his existence had been a mystery to her until just a few hours ago. She had been peeling parsnips and carrots for the soup when their father had burst through the back door.

"Set another place for dinner, Mother," Everett had said, grabbing his wife about the waist and hugging her close as she pushed the ham stuffing into the large turkey. "I've booked King David's room for Christmas."

Prudence shook her spoon at him. "Go along with you," she sternly admonished him, but her gray eyes under her graying head were dancing.

"Really, Pops?" Martha asked, setting down her paring knife in surprise, her dark blue eyes sparkling with interest; her tight chocolate curls bouncing with excitement; her round, pink face growing pinker with hope. "To whom?"

"Name's Abbott Simons," Everett said, as he released Prudence, and Martha's expression drooped. "Interesting chap. New York banker of the self-made sort. Met him at the general store when I ran over for tobacco. He's on his way to Hartford for a meeting and planned to sleep enroute in the coach, but I told him that was no way to spend Christmas when Spencer Inn was much more suitable. Oh, and by the way," Everett added, turning toward Martha. "A certain young fellow, oh say yonder high..."

Here, Everett raised his hand several inches above his head, and Martha blushed and turned away to hide her smile. "...with the most fetching brown eyes, dropped in while I was there. I took the liberty of inviting him to Christmas Eve dinner. You wouldn't be minding that, would you?"

Martha squealed with delight and leaped up to hug her father, upsetting the bowl of newly peeled potatoes.

"Now, lassie, you're neglecting your duties," Everett said, but he looked pleased as Martha scrambled to pick them up. "What'll I tell the guests tonight when there's no famous Spencer Inn fried potato balls on the table? Ralph," Everett said to Eleanor's fiancé, as clean-shaven as Everett but not nearly as stout, who was hauling up jugs of the inn's signature cider wine. "Unhitch my horses, there's a good fellow."

Lucetta smiled to herself as she added the vegetables to the giant soup kettles. She understood Everett's enthusiasm. She loved the old inn even more than her father did, if that was possible. With its high-beamed ceilings; wood interior of cedar and pine; red trim, colorful, hand-woven rugs; vases filled with dried native foliage; and original needlework draped across chair arms and backs, Spencer Inn lent a welcoming, if rustic, charm, unique to this part of rural Connecticut, where settlers valued stark practicality over style and grace. Lucetta hoped dinner preparations progressed smoothly. She hadn't quite finished stitching the lace on Eleanor's pillow, Lucetta's Christmas morning surprise for her eldest sister, as Lucetta had stuffed the pillow full of chamomile and feverfew to ease the severe headaches that often plagued Eleanor.

But it wasn't the inn, or even the pillow, now occupying Lucetta's thoughts. How could someone so successful be all by himself on Christmas Eve? Her heart warmed toward this man. She couldn't wait to meet him.

Everett saw to it as they bore the covered dishes of the Christmas Eve feast and lay them at the long rectangular table, topped in ivory damask, a table Everett's father Brinsley Spencer had built when he founded the inn at the turn of the century. Even more than the inn, Everett took enormous pride in the women of his household and showed them off at every available opportunity.

"Abbott," a beaming Everett said, bracing his left hand on his hip and giving his right hand a wide flourish. "These are my daughters: Eleanor, Lucetta, Martha, and Christine."

The man's expression did not change as his eyes probed the four young women who had stopped their activity to stand before him, from the thin-boned Eleanor with her flaxen hair neatly piled on the top of her regal head to Martha and then to the slightly plump Christine, who shared Martha's dark prettiness. But it was on Lucetta that Abbott's eyes lingered, and this made Lucetta's heart jump. Instinctively, she stood straighter, drawing attention to her already imposing figure. She was taller than everyone in her immediate family, and she had her father's large bones and light hair, except her thick mane hung in soft waves far past her waist.

12

"Girls," Prudence said in an impatient voice as she struggled to get both the turkey platter and her hoops through the dining room door. "I need your help serving."

At the sound of Prudence's voice, the smile on Everett's face vanished.

"What's the matter with you, standing around and letting your mother do all the work?" Everett said, but Lucetta heard the merriment in his voice, even as he pointed to the kitchen door. "Now, go!"

They scurried away to warm blue and white flowered Spode China and fill them with the table's bounties: vegetable soup and mutton soup, buttermilk corn bread and Irish soda bread with freshly churned butter and pounded cheese for spreading, pumpkin chips in syrup with cream for topping, "plum" pudding made with raisins and currants, and apple turnovers. The current guests filtered into the dining room and took their places. One was Charles Erler, bare scalp and bird's nest beard hanging six inches off his chin, who was traveling west to homestead. The elderly sisters, Miss Polly and Miss Fanny Moore, most of their jiggly flesh thankfully covered beneath black crepe, were heading to Wisconsin to keep house for their younger brother, a recent widower. The last were the newlyweds, Gunther and Gertrude Cook. Gunther was as silent during meals as Gertrude, who never smiled. Yet the pair made the most frightful noises at night and disturbed the sleep of the inn's other occupants.

Abbott Simons selected the chair opposite Lucetta's.

Her first clue into the psyche of this fascinating man came when Everett was reading from the Bible, his custom at the end of every dinner Lucetta had ever known.

"No room at the inn," Everett set the Bible on his lap with a contented sigh. "Girls, that's what makes our remote establishment so special. Every guest reminds us that the Lord God himself might make an appearance."

Prudence's head bobbed like a chicken over the teacups as she refilled them with her orange spice tea from one of the stainless steel serving pots.

"How hard it must be for our newest guest to be so far away from his family on Christmas Eve," Prudence said, sympathy in her moist eyes.

"Actually, this is my first family Christmas." Abbott looked at Lucetta as he said it. "I'm an orphan."

Prudence flushed at her error and stammered an apology, but Abbott held up his hand. "Please, ma'am, do not. T'is I who am beholden to you for your hospitality."

Christine, forgetting polite delicacy and her best table manners, blurted out, "So were you raised at the St. Joseph Orphanage for Boys?"

The St. Joseph Orphanage for Boys was a Hartford charity run by the Sisters of Mercy. They had gone there, once, to pass out bread during a diphtheria epidemic, as all four girls were immune. They had moved from cot to cot, aghast at all the pale faces, toddler eyes forever frozen wide in fear, blackened tongues and black-rimmed eyes, putrid brown ooze from flared nostrils that had lost the frantic battle for air, and the stench of post-mortem bowel movements.

Abbott gave a short laugh. "I wish to God I had. I ran away from my guardian when I was eight and lived off the streets."

"How awful!" Eleanor exclaimed, stirring sugar into her tea.

Abbott stared coolly at her. "Hunger and rats were preferable to thrice-daily beatings, ma'am." His eyes flickered to Lucetta and then back to Eleanor. "Again, I'm much obliged to your hospitality."

As guests moved to the parlor for the after-dinner festivities, the girls lagged behind to help Prudence remove the last traces of the dinner and tidy the kitchen. Eleanor began separating the food into a clay bowl, which she covered with a towel and handed to her mother.

"Girls, I'm just running over to Granny's," Prudence said. "I'll be right back."

A grim nightly ritual, for even on Christmas Eve, Granny Spencer would not join them. Everett's mother stood over six feet tall, but her crooked frame belied her height, wizened, wrinkled, and gnarled like the old Charter oaks surrounding her one room hut, about a mile north from the inn. After Brinsley's death, Granny had moved there - hers and Brinsley's first home during the inn's construction - declaring that her duties had ended and that she wouldn't be hog tied in performing any more of them. Granny had lived in the woods so long, few people in the nearby towns even recalled her existence. Still, Prudence insisted Granny was demented and should be forced to dwell in the main house with them, but Everett insisted his mother would do nothing of the kind. If Granny, after a long hard life of bearing fifteen children and burying eight of them, as well as four husbands, wanted to live in poverty and isolation, it was no one's business but hers. Surely, the least they could do was check on her from time to time and make sure she had decent food to eat. And Prudence, who really didn't want the queer old woman living in her house and sharing a room next to hers, conceded to Everett, because after all HE was the man of the house, and it was her God-given duty to follow his lead. With a grim smile and involuntary shudder, Lucetta lined up the leftovers for the ice box. The rest of the country avoided Granny, and the girls had made her the wicked witch in every childhood story they ever invented, the crone from which every jealous suitor solicited potions to claim the heart of his beloved. Still, for all her eccentricities, no abode matched

Granny's in cleanliness. No scraps of any kind. Everything went into the garden.

The fire burned cheerily in the parlor, gaily bedecked for Christmas with a Norway Pine standing in one corner (strung with popcorn, walnuts, and apples), and its leftover greenery from the trimming artfully arranged behind every painting. The room resounded with the rollicking notes of the yellowed piano keys, for her father played with an exuberance even experienced musicians couldn't top.

Martha's cheeks burned red from her proximity to the fireplace, the reflection of her calico holiday dress, and from standing next to Wyndham Franklin, wavy locks plastered to one side, wiry mustache waxed and curling to his chin, as he sipped cider wine and rambled about the Morgans he was breaking. Eleanor and Ralph sat on the Empire sofa, absorbed in demure conversation about heavens knew what. Eleanor had none of Martha's giddiness, but then, she and the soft-spoken Ralph would be married in the spring, so she had already adopted the soberness befitting a New England housewife and future proprietress of Spencer Inn.

"Come on, Lucy," Everett's voice rang out. "Play a tune with your dad and make an old man happy.

Delighted he had asked her, Lucetta settled beside him and banged out song after song: *Yankee Doodle, The Rich Lady O'er the Sea, When Love Gets You Fast in Her Clutches, Crazy Jane,* and *My Poor Dog Tray.* The old piano rang, with only minor interruptions from where D2 and B3 stuck and where the strings for C sharp and A flat were missing altogether. Everett always forgot this, so occasionally, a note went missing, which elicited a, "Damn incompetent piano tuner," from the man of the house and caused laughter to ripple across the room.

Mr. Erler set his glass on the top of the piano and leaned down. "Mr. Spencer, sir, your cider wine is first rate. Have you anymore?"

Everett threw back his head and laughed with a laughter that only happened after one too many glasses of his prized nectar, and he abruptly stopped playing with a final brisk succession of notes.

"Lucy," and Everett's voice slightly slurred as he spoke. "Keep the keys warm until your old dad comes back."

Feeling Abbot's eyes burn the back of her neck, Lucetta flipped through the Christmas songbook. She played, *O Tanenbaum, I Saw Three Ships Come Sailing In,* and was just beginning, *Good King Wenceslas* when she heard a voice close to her ear say, "Will you be playing all night?"

"Only until my father returns." Lucetta didn't have to glance over her shoulder to know the voice belonged to Abbott. She turned the page, praying she didn't skip a note in the process. She lacked her father's talent of playing by ear, but at least she could play. Everett had long ago abandoned the attempt with her sisters.

Lucetta was halfway through, *God Rest Ye Merry Gentlemen* when her father returned, happily quaffing a glass of cider and edging her off the piano bench. "Now, folks, I'll show you how we played *Deck the Halls* back in my day. Lucy, grab an eggnog and join the fun. You've been slaving away all day."

She stiffly rose from the piano bench, dismayed to see Abbott and Gunther in the far corner of the parlor and speaking in low tones. With her spirits sucked as dry as an old orange, Lucetta edged between old Miss Polly and the end of the larger sofa and pretended to enjoy a conversation about corns and smelling salts.

The grandfather clock down the hall solemnly struck midnight, and the party broke up. Everett, for all his joviality, was strict about bedtime, especially on Saturday and holidays. The traveling minister would be at the inn before dawn for services, and it was Everett's duty to ensure everyone was wide-eyed and ready for him.

But before they did, Everett insisted Lucetta play *Silent Night,* his favorite hymn and favorite way to conclude every Christmas Eve.

Lucetta had just reached the staircase when a gruff, "Ahem," behind her caused her to whirl around and face the stranger to whom she had yearned to speak all evening.

Abbott said, "Miss Lucetta, upon arriving at your inn, I found something lying outside. Do you believe in good luck?"

Lucetta blushed, but she stammered out, "Well, sir, I think that..."

But Abbot continued as if he hadn't noticed. "I believe eighteen-sixty will be a fine year. If you don't think it too forward of me..."

Here Abbott hesitated. "Miss Lucetta, please accept this from me as a symbol of my pleasure of having basked in your lovely company this evening."

Abbott pressed something cool and light into her palm, closed her fingers around it, and then, one by one, kissed her knuckles. He was gone before the astonished Lucetta could muster a response. Slowly, she opened her hand and stared at Abbott's gift. It was a six-leaf clover.

16

CHAPTER TWO: TASTING IMMORTALITY

Down,

    down,

       down,

          down,

             down into crackling tongues; and melting flesh; and writhing wisps; and shrieking shadows snapping like lion trainers' whips; and dazzling flames leaping, pirouetting, and chasing their tails with mad frenzy. In the inferno's center sat Satan, regal and unscathed, hair swept off his forehead and tangled in his thick horns, gray-blond strands sticking to his unlined face, as he tossed back his head and roared, "MUAHAHAHAHHAHAHAHAHAHAHAHAHAHAHAHAHAHA!
"Shhhh..."
John opened his eyes, pounding heart still racing. Gently, his mother lifted the damp locks from his wet cheeks and stroked his face with the back of her hand until the drumming in his chest slowed to easy, normal rhythms. The nursery fire burned low, tangerine and gold piercing the blackness. With a grunt, he struggled against the soggy weight pinning him to the feather mattress. She eased back the bedclothes, and he sprang upright, his arms already in the air, for they were well-accustomed to this nighttime routine. In a moment, she had peeled off the nightshirt; in the next, a second garment, cool and light, replaced the first. Water from the bedside pitcher trickled into a glass; she placed it to his parched lips, and he gulped the cold water. He watched her slender hands fluff the down pillows, and he sank against their billowy mounds as she drew up the covers and draped them around his waist.
"Mamma..."
"Go to sleep, Johnny."
Lucetta kissed his still-moist forehead and returned to her needlework. The black walnut rocker's even creak...creak...creak...creak...creak...creak...creak...eased his jangled nerves. For a time, he watched the needle glint in and out of the linen, until the nightmare relaxed its hold on his overtired mind and faded to gray. He rolled to one side and shifted his attention across the room and out the window. His star, spicules stretched to brilliant lengths in the midnight sky, stared back and twinkled, twinkled, twinkled. His tense limbs slackened; his eyelids drooped, blinked and blinked again; his mind wandered across fields of bluebells and daffodils. When John re-opened

his eyes, the early morning sun was casting pale beams across the burnished oak boards of the nursery floor, and Nurse was setting out his bread and milk and jam.

Sometimes John dreamed he had ascended the throne of God where he quaked before the mighty trumpet blasts as Yahweh himself, hair swept off his forehead, gray-blond strands brushing the collar of his snow-white garments, unrolled his lengthy scroll and roared the young penitent's many sins. It didn't matter if John dreamed of his father as the devil or the Almighty, for behind the walls of the Fifth Avenue mansion loosely called "home," John perceived Farlow Abbott Simons as the embodiment of omnipotence, supreme authority, and judgment, an eternal presence John could never please.

On Sundays and Holy Days of Obligation when Abbot stayed in town, father and son attended High Mass at St. Patrick's Cathedral, its Federal-style architecture and plaster ceiling and walls inside its one hundred and twenty-foot-long and fifty-foot-wide interior resembling home: hard, beautiful, and cold. As erect and immobile as the marble statues, but not nearly so tall, Abbot stood beside his son, and, to the accompaniment of the Erben organ, sang those majestic Latin hymns in a strong and powerful tenor voice.

John even recalled the first day they had attended: March seventeenth, eighteen-sixty-eight. The sermon, delivered by Archbishop John McClosky, droned on and on and on. More than once, a restless John shuffled his feet and felt his father's pinch.

"He speaks too much," John whispered after one such assault on his neck.

Abbot did not reply, but during the walk home, Abbott did say, "A fire destroyed the sanctuary two years ago, but, as you saw today, it was rebuilt. The archbishop will not always talk so long. Today was the cathedral's rededication, the feast day of the church's' patron saint."

John had opened his mouth to ask, "What's a patron saint?" But Abbot had chosen that moment to toss a coin at a ragged boy with a runny nose in exchange for a copy of the New York Gazette, and John let the question drift away.

Often, as John stole glances at his father lifting his voice to the firmament in song, he wondered if the beautiful words cut into Abbot's alabaster exterior to stir something of the immortal within him, or if his father merely crooned empty syllables. Sometimes after Mass, Abbott would walk through the church's cemetery, pausing now and again before a tombstone, and bowing his head in prayer.

Certainly, heaven had nothing on home. Long before John approached his father's height, he had learned the secret of his father's influence and prominence: money and plenty of it. One decided

18

advantage to perceiving Abbot as God the Father was it made John the beloved son, with each servant underneath the roof of the Beaux Arts structure catering to John's every quirk and caprice. By the time John could toddle on two feet, he had discovered Nurse would scuttle if he snapped his fingers, whether he desired a reading from Mother Goose or Grimm's fairy tales; a block fortress built; or a hop, skip, and a jump across upper Manhattan's busy sidewalks; the household servants stepped aside when John trotted through the hall, even as they hastened to open doors for the junior master; and a plate toppled in displeasure caused Cook to whip up another dinner more suitable, or, even better, send his mother into the kitchen to cook a custom meal.

Because if Abbott was King of Kings and Lord of Lords and his castle the celestial palace, Lucetta was the personification of the Creator's grace and mercy, the angel moving about his world bestowing pure love.

On Cook's day off, she hand-prepared and hand-fed her son meals of a delicacy Cook could never hope to attain, seasoned with a mysterious combination of flavorings she grew in her chambers, transplanted from Granny Spencer's garden.

Standing on a chair, cheek resting on a hand, John watched Lucetta's delicate fingers as she chopped, sliced, dumped, and mixed, sprinkling each entree, soup, and bakery with her special blend of seasonings. Afterwards, mother and son would depart to a remote alcove of the house, Lucetta to sip orange-spiced tea and John to devour those servings of one under her watchful and loving eye.

"Only for you, Johnny," Lucetta would say in a kind and soothing voice as she fondled his hair. "Only for you."

On the rare occasions John fell ill, Lucetta herself nursed him back to health, again with a concoction of herbs from her indoor garden. When he felt sad, tired or out of sorts, she brought him back to himself with soft words and even softer caresses, as he rested against her bosom, stared out the window, and meditated on his star.

He had asked her once, as she knelt beside him at the side of his bed while he recited his prayers.

"Mamma," John said, pausing between, "Holy Mary, Mother of God" and "Pray for us sinners."

"Yes, Johnny," Lucetta, had answered, glancing down at the earnest face gazing up at hers.

"What is that?" And John pointed to the sparkling sentinel star.

Lucetta's face had softened, and she had caressed the blond head for many minutes before speaking.

"That, Johnny," Lucetta kissed his locks, "is your sister in heaven."

John watched the star wax and wane with their words. "I have a sister in heaven?" And he thought of the seraphim and cherubim, the glorious antiphons they ceaselessly sang, and the fact he had a sibling lucky enough to hear divine refrains.

"Yes, a beautiful, angelic sister who is always keeping watch over you. Wherever you roam, and whatever you do, your sister will accompany you."

Mostly, however, John knew music, from the cathedral's Gregorian chant to the waltzes hired musicians played at his parents' parties, to the Irish folk songs Nurse crooned as she straightened the nursery, and the hymns his mother hummed as she rocked and sewed. Even more, John understood life had its own tune, rhythm, beat, an exciting dance of stressed and unstressed syllables.

There was the rolling drudrudrudrudrudru of morning carriages across Fifth Avenue; the tchew, tchew-tchew of Java sparrows in Central Park, the fuooooooooooo, fuooooooooooo, fuooooooooooo of the wind against the glass on a March day and this same wind - angry, fierce, and screeching - during a summer thunderstorm when bass rocked the skies and lightning thhhhhhhhhhhited its admiration; the blubble, blubble, blubble of his bath water as Nurse poured it from pitcher to tub and the clattering of his own water into a chamber pot, also held by Nurse, breaking the house's still quiet in the middle of the night; and the pitter-pitter-splat, pitter-splat, pitter, patter- patter-patter of autumn rain against the house. Walking up and down the great staircase mimicked the increase and decrease of what Lucetta called the C-major scale, the squeak of chalk on his slate rivaled the highest of end notes; and even getting dressed had its musical syllables: arm in; arm in; shirt over head; button, button, button up.

And in the arrangement of these notes and chords and trebles and clefs, John discovered the secret of his own godliness before he could count to one hundred or recite his ABC's.

As always, John and his mother had spent the summer at Spencer Inn, his grandparents' establishment in rural Connecticut. The miracle had occurred soon after he and Lucetta had returned from bringing Granny Spencer her dinner, which they had laid on the floor in her doorway of her dilapidated hut, so Granny could shove her face into the slop and gobble it from all fours, as was her habit. Granny had just begun to feed, and John and Lucetta had just turned to leave when a trailing vine, its curling tendrils woven among the foliage and wound to the top of the old Charter oaks, caught John's interest. The leaves were simple, triangular and lobed; its tiny flowers were white; its berries were black and shiny. Mesmerized, John reached out to further examine it when Granny sprang like a panther and knocked him to the ground.

"Bryony!" she screeched, her nose touching his, as the boy screamed in terror and pain.

20

Lucetta's hands dove into his armpits, and she tried hauling him to his feet, but Granny's talons clawed into his neck as she spat, "Poison!"

With a hard tug, Lucetta extricated John from Granny's grasp, leaving Granny sitting on the ground, muttering and yanking out handfuls of grass and sprinkling them over her head. John shook like bryony leaves in a gale all the way back to the inn, even though his mother kept a firm grasp on him and murmured, "There, there," with an occasional anxious backward glance. But solicitudes didn't stop the smarting of his wounds, made all the more painful as John swiped at the blood that, despite his valiant efforts, trickled down his neck and under his collar.

Mama Prudie had met them at the kitchen door with a gasp and a distressed, "Oh, my," leaving the rest of the post-dinner cleanup to the aunties, so she could bathe John's neck with lye soap and cover it with one of Lucetta's soothing herbal salves.

Tending to John's gashes took so long that Papa Everett was halfway into his evening piano recital before John and his mother joined the other guests in the spacious parlor. Papa Everett sang, *Blue-eyed Jane*, and the men folk chimed in with *Ho! Westward Ho*. Uncle Ralph came back from tending the stock and joined them for the last chorus of *When Johnny Comes Marching Home Again*, nudging and winking at John as he sang. Auntie Eleanor sat in front of the tiered corner shelf and knitted a sweater for Uncle Ralph, her foot keeping time to the music springing from Everett's fingers. Auntie Martha didn't participate, but, then, Auntie Martha, who dressed in black crepe, never sang and rarely spoke. By day, Auntie Martha wordlessly completed her household duties; by night she retreated to the Book of Common Prayer, lips moving in silent petitions.

"Come on, Lucy," Papa Everett's voice rang out, "Play a tune with your dad and make an old man happy."

A pink flush crept into his mother's cheeks and her already happy smile broadened into a happier one as she joined Papa Everett at the piano bench. John often sat by Lucetta when she played in the drawing room at home, but those doleful strains contrasted wildly with the spirited music filling the parlor. Together Papa Everett and Lucetta sang, *Willie Bell*, and *My Grandfather Had Some Very Fine Ducks*, and *Were I Poss'd of Fairy Pow'r,* and the parlor resounded with the tunes those old keys produced, making John's fingers tingle their reverberations.

As Papa Everett completed *Away for the Country,* adding a few additional chords of his own, John announced in a clear childish voice, "You missed."

A pause, and Papa Everett turned around. "I missed? What did I miss?"

John scampered to the piano and played a perfect C#m7b9.
"This," John said.

Papa Everett watched him, stunned.

"My word, Lucy," Papa Everett faced his daughter. "Have you been teaching the lad?"

Open-mouthed and wide-eyed, Lucetta shook her head. An everlasting moment passed as Papa Everett, head low, thought. A moment later, Papa Everett jumped to his feet, lifted John, and set him on the empty place.

"Go on, Johnny," Papa Everett smiled encouragingly. "Play another."

John stared at the keys and at the unfamiliar notations written in the propped-up book above him.

"I don't know any," John said.

Papa Everett gave John's head an uncertain, but friendly pat. "Then simply play."

The songs always bursting inside exploded. From his fingers flowed the tunes and arias he'd heard at home, but also the ones he heard inside his head: rainbows after a midday storms, violets growing in Lucetta's chamber, tingling fingers after a snowy walk, vanilla ice cream on a balmy summer afternoon, the first lighting of Christmas candles, popcorn jumping in a Spencer Inn kettle...

Finally, Lucetta gently pried his fingers from the keys, saying, "It's well past bedtime, Johnny," and shut the lid. John's little body sagged, and if Lucetta hadn't caught and cradled him in her arms, he might have toppled to the floor. The parlor was empty, save for Papa Everett dozing in the overstuffed chair by the cold fireplace. Lucetta carried John up the staircase, down the hall, and past the row of bedrooms. As they passed the second floor sitting room's bay window, Lucetta shielded John's eyes, but not before he caught a glimpse of Granny cavorting naked beneath an Aurelian moon.

Far into the night, John lay, hands clasped behind his neck, and listened to the melodies in his mind while his star sparkled back. He thought of his sister in heaven and tried to imagine the angelic alleluias forming her reality. An owl hooted; Granny screeched back; and a bat flapped past his window. Lucetta stirred next to him and rolled onto her side. His star moved closer and stretched its arms until it resembled the starfish Nurse had shown him in the great big picture book of...

For the remainder of the summer, Papa Everett gave John free and full access to the piano, all day and every day. Before sunup until well past sundown, John played, ignoring both hunger and thirst until he teetered on the bench. Twice he fainted from lack of sustenance - which Lucetta remedied with savory meals she hand-prepared and delivered to the piano - and more than once, John, breeches already damp, dashed to the outhouse.

One sultry August afternoon, Lucetta insisted he break from the piano, so John, Lucetta and the aunties had spent the afternoon exploring the cool woods beyond the inn, where patches of light escaped the packed tree tops. His mother and Auntie Eleanor gathered bouquets of blue wood asters and purple gentians; Auntie Martha's black crepe swished through tall grasses; and John experimented with oak, black maple and hawthorn leaf whistles, varying their tone and pitch.

Late afternoon, they stopped at Granny's to refresh themselves with tea and scones, which Granny baked over an open fire and flavored with rosemary and thyme from her garden. Her dank cabin boasted her handiwork: crude pottery stacked like nesting cups in one corner; wooden buckets of various sizes dumped in another; coils of rope scattered on the floor like fibrous cobras. Each herb and flowering plant from the Garden of Eden draped across the walls like overdone Christmas garland and hung from the ceiling like common tree snakes. Soon, John's face felt grimy from the loose dirt Granny was kicking up from the earth floor as she whisked about the abode, leaping high and knocking her bare heels together, while preparing the simple refreshments.

After some lighthearted gossip to which even Granny contributed a well-timed cackle or snort, Granny divined their fortunes from the sage leaves in their empty cups. In Auntie Eleanor's, Granny read, "a letter bearing good news" and in Auntie Martha's, "romance," and in his mother's, "a trip abroad."

But when Granny peered inside at John's viney pattern, spiraling from base to lip, she knocked the clay vessel to the ground, smashed it in a two-footed single stomp, and screeched, "Out! Out! Out! Out!"

The little party didn't need to be ordered twice. They fled.

Not until late August, after John and his mother had bid the grandparents and aunties good-bye - with smothering hugs and declarations of returning next summer - and had settled into the plush cushions of the chugging locomotive from New Haven to New York, did Lucetta whisper in his ear, "You must not speak to your father about playing the piano."

John considered her words, not yet comprehending how making music was a quality inherent to him and not part of the magical atmosphere of the Connecticut countryside.

Lucetta shook his shoulder. "Johnny, did you hear me?"

Startled, John glanced up at his mother. Her cheeks were flushed; her eyes were flashing. Uneasy, he pulled back slightly, but she gripped tighter.

"You must promise me," she insisted quietly.

As if John ever perched on his father's knee and shared his heart. Wary of his mother's vehemence, John slowly, thoughtfully, nodded.

"I promise, Mamma."

John's life assumed a regular rhythm: New York winters as frigid and predictable as his home environment followed by Connecticut summers, replete with warm sunshine and country meals served on Spode China blue and white flowered dishes, so different from the multi-course feasts served under lids at home.

He savored Papa Everett's sausage (flavored with black and cayenne peppers and brown and maple sugar) accompanied by Mama Prudie's flannel cakes and spiced pear butter topping for breakfast; sourdough biscuits and beef gravy poured over roasted potatoes for lunch; and boiled turnips, stewed squashes, baked beans and the succulent flesh of squab or rabbit for dinner, with shortcakes and wild blueberries for dessert.

Most importantly, while Uncle Ralph and the hired men tended the extensive gardens; and his mother, Mama Prudie, and the aunties stewed and canned tomatoes, dried apples and berries in the sun for next winter, soaked rennet and chopped curd for cheese; and churned sweet cream into butter, or, even better, made ice cream, Papa Everett drank coffee and munched thick slices of molasses cake while teaching him to read music.

"Here is middle C," Papa Everett said, left corner of his mouth drooping, his voice slurring, a permanent reminder of last winter's attack of apoplexy. He gave "C" a single hard plunk. "And here," he added, fingers skipping right, "are the nineteen treble clef notes, while over there," and Papa Everett's fingers dribbled left, "are the nineteen bass clef notes."

John wriggled at the sound of these rippling spirits and his formal introduction to them.

"Now, Johnny, these notes have names." Papa Everett identified them as his fingers produced their individual tones. "Now you try." He removed his pocket handkerchief and dabbed away crumbs and coffee-tinged drool from his numb chin.

John played the notes, his index finger delighting in each sound, and identifying aloud as they rang out.

Papa Everett beamed his approval with a crooked smile and reached for the open songbook. Several sheets slid to the floor. John started to retrieve them, but Papa Everett eased John back by his starched high collar. "Never mind them, Johnny. Look. Do you see the face?"

Leaning forward and biting the tip of his tongue in concentration, John studied the faded black marks. Moments later, his face brightened.

"I do," John touched each note. "F. A. C. E."

He looked to his grandfather for validation, but Papa Everett was calling out, "Mother, oh, Mother!"

24

John slid off the bench and snatched the runaway pages. Mama Prudie scurried into the parlor, wiping her hands across her apron at the moment he emerged from under the piano.

"Yes, dear?" She stopped as the music began, John playing George Arthur Barker's *Llewelyn's Bride* without a single mistake.

Papa Everett turned red and slid the sheet behind the songbook.

"That's one you can play when you're a little older," Papa Everett said with nervous laugh and quick clearing of his throat. He flipped through the book. "Try this one."

John launched into a perfect execution of *Amazing Grace.*

"See, Mother? He's a born musician."

"Yes, indeedy," Mama Prudie smoothed back the gray hairs escaping her bun. "Why, he's..."

"Be right back, Johnny," Papa Everett stood, eyeing his coffee cup and grabbing his cane. "Need a refill. Mother, any more cake?"

In September, John partook, for the first time, of true immortality, which strengthened both his soul and his resolve for the next chapter in his life. Kneeling at the thick oak Communion rails in a new white suit - Abbot's concession to Lucetta as black was the custom - white carnation at the lapel and matching white kid gloves, John squeezed his eyes shut and quivered at the impending moment, the consuming of Jesus Christ's actual body and blood, placed into his mouth from the hands of the squinting and never-smiling archbishop standing before him in heavy white and gold vestments.

"Corpus Christi," Father McClosky droned. "Sanguis Christi."

And John opened his mouth for his portion of holy bread and wine.

The following summer, John tasted his first success. Spencer Inn swelled its ranks on weekends, for visitors from two counties out had heard of the accomplished young pianist and made the short jaunt to prove the veracity of the rumors. Papa Everett, cider wine in hand and good-natured as always, abandoned his post at the piano, played hospitable host, and displayed his only grandchild's musical aptitude to men in vested suits and splendid pocket watches hanging by sterling chains and woman with plaited hair and brooches clasped to their lace collars.

"My word, Spencer, the boy is a chip off the old block," one man slurred, the ends of his bulky dark mustache wet with cider wine. "You sure his instruction didn't begin at birth?"

Papa Everett chuckled as he leaned on his cane as he exchanged his own glass for the decanter.

"Just a natural feel for the instrument," Papa Everett said as he refilled the man's glass. "Sometimes I think the boy should be teaching me." He turned to the slender woman standing next to him. "Ma'am?"

The man's wife also held out her glass, but her gaze stayed on John, who hovered over the keys and immersed the room with dazzling airs.

"So serious," the woman marveled. "I shan't but wonder if something t'will come of it."

"When it happens," Papa Everett said, tipping the last drops into the empty glass of a passerby. "I'll retire to my inn and spend the remainder of my days enjoying my guests and my nights being entertained by Johnny."

A far less encouraging welcome had greeted John upon the return trip to New York. News of John's miniature concerts traveled to Abbott's ears, and he bristled at the fact Lucetta had allowed the future president of F.A. Simons & Company to entertain peasants at the risk of the family's good name. John had heard his father's outrage from his mother's adjacent chambers as he arranged his blocks in a semicircle on the nursery floor: the largest in the middle and the rest as a miniature audience to the genius composer/pianist in its midst.

"The boy needs formal studies in grammar, mathematics, and rhetoric! I guarantee it, Lucetta, I shall engage a tutor before the week is up!"

"The boy has a gift! Nurture it, I beg you!"

"Get your hand off me, or I'll..."

"Please reconsider...Abbott, no!"

A loud thunk, a louder cry from Lucetta, a slamming of the door, and silence, except for his mother's anguished sobbing. John, head hanging and block in hand, rolled sinister eyes toward the wall. The bubble of enthrallment in which John had dwelled the last three months popped, and it was his father who inserted the lance. He slammed the block onto the other wood patrons in the mezzanine, leaped to his feet, viciously kicked the remaining blocks across the nursery floor, and mentally drew his sword. By voicing vehement disapproval to John's music, Abbot became a permanent rival against his son. John had neither the height nor power to oppose his father, but that day would arrive, and when it did, Abbot would beg for scraps from John's enormous banquet table and lick the soot from John's Wellington boots.

In the meantime, John would steer himself toward the business of beginning his own kingdom and his own legacy, one that did not include, now and forever, the need for his father's position and money.

CHAPTER THREE: KEYS TO HEAVEN

John never practiced while his father was in the house, and rarely when he was in town, but John bided his time, waiting for Abbott's departure for a long bank meeting, or even longer business trip, when he could seize the drawing room and fill it with compositions in progress.

All his impressions, experienced but not expressed, John now translated into notes and cadences. Something awakened in his soul and keenly enlivened him during those many hours sitting at the polished Brazilian rosewood of the Steinway grand in the center of the enormous first floor drawing room.

Abbott favored this room for parties, as it boasted a marble fireplace; gold leaf and hand-painted wallpaper; mahogany furniture; and over one hundred original pieces of fine art: busts, as well as large oils in heavy gold frames. He had strictly forbidden John's entry unless accompanied by either him or Lucetta. But John, too, favored the room, for its high vaulted ceilings had terrific acoustics; its remote location confined the music to the east wing.

Always, John spurned his mother's hymnal on its carved rack in favor of the music dwelling in his psyche. During his father's ever increasingly frequent absences, John obsessively played all day and well into the night, and only with the greatest reluctance could Nurse's threats of future beatings when his father returned home coax him to take his bath, eat his dinner, or work his sums. Bedtime, whenever it arrived, always arrived too early. John would lie awake, serenaded by the music inside his head, until Nurse began snoring over her darning needle. That's when John crept away into the drawing room and pounded the keys until an indignant Nurse interrupted the revelry of his soaring emotions and rudely pulled him away.

Each chord played deepened the wedge between Abbott and John, for Abbott appeared to understand only finances, and John grew more determined not to lose his soul to the counting house as his father had. This poison of tallies and figures had spread to his mother, for Lucetta moved more slowly and with greater lethargy, an ethereal presence even in her own suite, as she cared for, and murmured softly to, her beloved and rapidly multiplying houseplants. As John became more introspective, Lucetta became more reclusive and less attentive to her son, an emotional invalid in her other-worldly sanctuary of flowers, herbs, fine furnishings and pastels, whereas John flourished in his own reality. His music grew richer; his imagination became more vivid; and each original arrangement fueled the fire burning hotter day by day.

"Master John, did you hear me?"

The orchestra stopped. John beheld, not ivory and ebony but page seventy-six of *Harvey's Elementary Grammar and Composition.* His tutor, Mr. Andrew Helsby from lower Manhattan, a foppish sort in corduroy jacket, well-coiffured tower of scented curls, and homespun breeches tucked inside a sturdy set of boots, rapped his pointer against the chalkboard.

"I did."

"Then please parse the next sentence."

Fortunately, binary logarithms; ethos, pathos, and logos; and "parlez vous francais" also came easily to John, so, except for occasional slips in his young charge's concentration, necessitating stern reminders to the present task, Mr. Helsby easily earned his rather generous annual salary of two thousand dollars.

As John's classical knowledge grew, so did his height and hair. John noted with fiendish satisfaction he now stood an inch taller than the current ruling Simons and the strands topping his father's head had grown white and sparse. For this reason, John delighted in allowing his mane to run long and wild during Connecticut summers, replete with unregulated music, his mother's and Mama Prudie's delectable country meals, and equestrian lessons with Uncle Ralph, a first-rate horseman. When formal training had ended, uncle and nephew roamed the lush verdure, and John reveled in the clean air, distant groves and hills, and the horse's stride between his legs. Later and in silence, for Uncle Ralph was not loquacious, they cleaned the stalls, distributed oats, and brushed the drafts and thoroughbreds until they gleamed.

Upon John's return home to the city, he once again submitted to the shears. With smug gratification, John watched each abundant lock as it dropped onto his father's treasured Persian rugs.

One evening, Nurse hustled the eleven-year-old John out of his bath, re-dressed him in breeches and a starched ruffled shirt and hurried him down the stairs, with John resisting all the way.

"Why the fuss?" John asked, interest piqued once he realized they were heading to the drawing room.

"Your father sent for you," Nurse said in an excited whisper.

Nurse abandoned him at the drawing room door, which she shut behind him. In a haze of Havana smoke gathered New York's financial moguls flanked by their tightly laced wives, and these women, in their House of Worth gowns, simultaneously and disapprovingly, raised their lorgnettes at the boy's intrusion into their society.

Abbott noticed John standing in the foyer. As Charles refilled the brandy glass in Abbott's outstretched hand, Abbott said to his guests, "Here's the boy. John, demonstrate your prowess."

The longest gaze in history passed between father and son. Then John gave a half-bow and approached the piano. A murmur ran through the crowd, but John waited for his father's nod before he allowed his fingers, aching with the need to flaunt their genius, touch the beloved instrument. Permission granted, John played a prelude, and then an etude and then a waltz, and then a mazurka, and then a nocturne, and then a polonaise, and then a serenade, and then a scherzo, and then a ballade, and then parts of his sonata and his concerto in progress. John was fully cognizant of the reaction his music had on the regal crowd. A touch of the keys here, a hard pressing of the keys there - the oh-so wonderful up and down manipulation of the magnificent whites and blacks - also manipulated these men and women far more than any of his father's sumptuous feasts ever could. With a few finger movements, they smiled; they cried; they sighed their pleasure; and John now knew, with absolute certainty, he had harnessed something more commanding than money.

One gentleman, his face as wrinkled as a forgotten prune in the cellar of Spencer Inn, tapped the ashes from his cigar onto the rug and exclaimed, "Extraordinary! Who is the composer for that last piece?"

John ceased the rhapsody.

"I am," he said.

"What impertinence!"

His buxom bride, still clinging to his arm, tittered into her glass and sloshed its contents onto his trousers. Abbott flushed, took a large step forward, a hesitant step backward, and spluttered, "You're...dismissed!"

Slowly, John rose to his full height, He first faced his father and then bid the party farewell with a second half-bow. He strode out of the room, thunking Nurse in the forehead with the door, where she crouched behind it, eavesdropping. She scolded him for his boast all the way up to the nursery, but as John lay in bed later that night and contemplated his star, it twinkled back approval, and he drifted into peaceful sleep.

His slumber was broken several hours later by his father charging into the room. John blinked awake to the sight of Abbott, wild-eyed, crimson-red, and holding his crop over John's head. The serene dispassion in John's eyes clearly unsettled Abbott, because instead of striking, Abbot shouted, "I'm giving you one last chance, you scamp! Who wrote it?"

John met his father's frenzy with a calm and steady stare.

"I did," he said softly.

For the first time in his young life, John watched his father's face crumple. Abbott lowered the crop, looked away, and demanded in a low voice, "Have you written others?"

"Yes, sir."

Abbott stumbled to Lucetta's rocker and fumbled for the cord. Mission fulfilled, Abbott's head dropped against the chair. John swore a quiver ran through his father.

Charles, dragging the sash of his robe across the floor, scurried in with a glass and scurried out. Abbot took a sip, whispered, "You will play them for me," and then knocked back the rest of the drink.

"Yes, sir."

Fortified by whiskey, for it was too early in the day for brandy, Abbott led the way to the drawing room with John's bare feet tripping over his nightshirt as he hurried to keep pace. The moment John entered, Abbot whirled around, grabbed John's ear, and pulled him to the piano bench.

"Play, damn it!"

John played song after song after song for his father, who sagged against the piano, face in his hands. At the end of the etude, a voice behind John cleared his throat. Abbott dropped his hands and stood straight. John stopped playing and peeked over his shoulder. Prune-face had also witnessed the mini concert.

"The boy's talent is obvious." The man frowned. "Abbott, you'd be a fool not to develop it."

Abbott scowled and walked away.

"I know the perfect instructor. Ever hear of Seymour Cassidy?"

A finger jabbed John mid-back, and Abbot barked, "Keep playing." To his companion, Abbott added, "The European master?"

"The very same."

John switched from fortissimo to pianissimo and pretended to be engrossed in his hand movements.

"I thought he had retired," Abbott said.

"From performance, yes. But he wishes to continue his legacy, so he accepts a few pupils he believes have potential."

"You are acquainted with Mr. Cassidy?"

"Well, not personally. But we know someone who is."

"Who?"

"Lord Girard."

A pause. "I see."

"I'll send word this very day."

"Fine."

Abbott rang for Charles.

A month later, John and Helsby were crossing the main staircase on their way to the library, when the front doorbell rang.

"Wait," John said.

Helsby stopped, puzzled, then his face brightened.

"Ah, yes, I almost forgot," Helsby said. "Your father is interviewing Mr. Cassidy today."

The door opened and a slouched man, slight in height and stout in width, about seventy, and wrapped in a full cape, handed Gibbs his wide-brimmed hat, swiped the door knob with a gloved finger, and scornfully appraised the room.

Behind John, Helsby sucked in his breath.

"I envy you, Master John. Rumor has it he's brilliant. Oh, if I could shake hands with him."

"You shake hands for me. I don't like him, and neither will my father. Let's go."

But Helsby, face aglow, hung over the banister, delighting in the downstairs scene just out of reach to him.

John leaned into his tutor.

"Go ahead, Helsby," John said in a low voice. "Feast upon his appearance and draw out your pleasure, for I've no doubt we've seen the last of him."

John's formal music lessons began the following week, intensifying John's dislike of Maestro, the sole title Seymour Cassidy expected to hear from his new pupil. John could tolerate Maestro's crusty arrogance, heavy jowls, shaggy white eyebrows, a back as curved as middle C, a mouth frozen in a permanent frown, and even the ruler kissing John's knuckles whenever he made a mistake, and John made many for Maestro eschewed John's creative wanderings and insisted he stick to the curriculum.

This last crossed John's line of tolerance.

"You don't want a successor," John sneered as Maestro scorned another dash of originality. "You want an automaton."

Down slapped the ruler.

"You may fancy yourself a master once you compose your own celebrated *Missa solemnis*," Maestro replied as John shook his smarting hand. "Until then, add your embellishments to what you play best, the scales."

Ironically, these lessons from Seymour Cassidy came with a caveat from his father.

"Neglect your studies," Abbott had warned when he informed John he had a music teacher, "and I'll terminate him."

The temptation was delicious, but John had already pledged to become his father's superior in all disciplines. With such a lofty goal spurring him along, John threw himself into his schoolwork with the same frenzy he gave the piano. The best part? John no longer needed to sneak into the drawing room to play, for his father had granted his musical muse free expression, except during the hours John played under Maestro's clutches.

31

WHACK!

John drew back his right hand and rubbed it with his left. "I doubt you'd smack Mozart."

"Mozart was a genius," Maestro said. "You are not."

John glared at Maestro, but he turned the page. "Mozart began composing at five. I played full symphonies in my head long before that age."

"My deepest sympathies."

"Look, Mozart invented his own style."

"Dare you pretend to know more than the masters?"

Before John could counterattack, the ruler did it for him.

That summer, John stayed home, for Lucetta, mind wandering, didn't remember to go, and Abbott refused to allow John to travel without her. John felt mild, if any, disappointment, for he now had his music in New York, especially after Maestro and Helsby left for the day.

The following June brought bad news: a telegram from Auntie Eleanor announcing the unexpected death of Mama Prudie and insisting Lucetta and John be dispatched on the next train to New Haven. Abbott shared the news with John over breakfast the next morning.

John choked, hastily set down his coffee, and slid the napkin from its porcelain ring.

"You never told them?" John spluttered.

"No reason to tell them." Abbot sliced into his ham, raised a forkful to his mouth, noticed John's indigence, and lowered it again.

"Fine, I did mention she was ill and under the care of New York's finest physicians." Abbott reached for the peppermill and gave his omelet a generous sprinkling. "Do you think me a scoundrel? I can't fix it; they can't fix it. It's kinder this way."

"So I'm staying home?" John returned to his breakfast. Nurse had retired to her sister's Boston home before Easter, so even that option was not available to him.

"No, you're leaving tomorrow. Helsby will accompany you."

That news put John in fine humor for the rest of the day, as it meant he could play for a week or so without Maestro's hindrance. So when Maestro interspersed the lesson with criticisms of John's technique, John repressed the scathing remarks and just once inquired, "What do you suggest?"

"I suggest practice."

"Further practice is impossible," John retorted, without missing a note. "I doubt even you can add hours to the day."

Maestro picked up John's hand, and the music ended in a discordant cacophony.

"I see no blood," Maestro said, turning the hand over and studying it. "Merely the soft skin of a noblewoman." He let the hand drop.

"Stuff your credentials and your outdated methods. You're merely an egotist, nothing more, nothing less."

"And you, Master John, don't want virtuosity badly enough."

Interestingly, the ruler had nothing to add.

The next day, standing on the bustling terminal, John had to remind himself that the reason behind the journey was a grim one, so elated was he at freedom from Maestro's admonishments. Beside him, Helsby carried the lunch box in one hand, the large water jar in the other, and the morning edition of the New York Gazette under one arm.

Grinning and gazing around him, Helsby puffed out his chest, inhaled deeply, and exclaimed, "What a perfect day for an excursion!"

The locomotive responded with a loud hiss of steam. John glanced at his tutor. Helsby's eyes danced as they roamed about the platform. John couldn't understand such animation for a simple four-hour jaunt until a sudden thought came to him.

"Ever ride on a train, Helsby?"

Still smiling, Helsby bent close to John's ear.

"Never." A giggle escaped Helsby lips, and he masked it with a cough. "First time."

"Well, man, pull yourself together," John whispered, looking around with a sharp eye. "It's undignified."

But Helsby's fascination continued as they boarded the train. He bowed at everyone he passed and ran his hands over the chair fabrics once they had settled in their seats. The second the train pulled out of the station, Helsby assumed the role of town crier.

"Master John, listen to this. The attorney general has asked the treasury for accounts Brigham Young filed twelve years ago."

John said nothing. He'd read it in yesterday's evening edition.

"Illegal trading with Indians, it seems." Helsby turned a page. "Railroad laborers are considering striking."

John stifled an irritated sigh and turned his attention to the blurring tracks.

"Wages cut again."

"I heard."

A rustling of paper, silence, and then Helsby's voice rang out, "Edison's done it again, invented a machine that talks."

"I know."

"Ah!

He nudged John's shoulder and held out the newspaper for John to see. Perplexed, John read, "Officials in Washington want to offer Sitting Bull immunity?"

Helsby's face fell, and he tapped an advertisement. "*This* one."

"Grand concert by the celebrated Gilmore Brass Band. Every Sunday afternoon. Free admission.'" John pushed the newspaper away. "Who cares?"

"I care. I can take my girl."

The insult John prepared to level against the celebrated Gilmore and his Brass Band died on his lips. Domestics lived a separate life outside their service to the household? Stunned, John regarded his tutor with this fresh insight.

"You have a girl, Helsby?

"I do. And her father lets me see her every Sunday afternoon."

"Well, good for you," John said with a short laugh. Imagine that. Helsby. In love. With a girl.

"Thank you." Helsby turned another page. "A Pictorial History of the World. Six hundred and seventy-two fine engravings.' How I long to own this book."

"Why?"

An image rose in John's mind of the library at home, a large room with thousands of titles. It had never occurred to John to buy a book. When he wanted one to read, he walked to the west wing and selected one.

"What do you mean, 'why?' I like to learn things. Don't you?"

"I should think you'd want to abandon the schoolmaster's role for a spell."

"It's not about a role. It's curiosity about the world. If I had the money, I'd send for a copy straight away."

"So do it." John once again turned his attention to the window. "My father pays you generously."

"I couldn't possibly, not in good conscience."

"Why not?"

"My pay goes to Mums. Father ran away six years ago, and she's not in good health."

Stunned again, John faced Helsby. "You're supporting a family?"

"Only until my younger brother is old enough for charity school. Then Mums will return to Rhode Island. She still has family there."

"You say it so casually." John thought of Lucetta, alone in her chambers, talking to plants, and the fact he would no longer take a trip under her care. "Won't you...?"

"Miss her? Certainly, but it's preferable to her dying in a tenement."

Truth, as John knew truth, peeled back its layers to reveal another truth, stark and blunt. Beneath the worn clothes in the adjacent chair lived an actual man, one with hopes and dreams and longings and aspirations.

34

John reflected on the financial empire Abbott had built and the musical one he was constructing. He couldn't imagine applying Herculean effort toward teaching.

"But...tutoring? Why Helsby?"

"The money, of course...and a natural aptitude for it, I suppose. Before working for your father, I served as headmaster for a small school in Cooperstown."

Helsby folded the newspaper, slid it down the arm chair, and reached for the lunch tin on the floor.

"Well, I'm famished." Helsby opened the box and tipped it toward John. "Sandwich?"

John shook his head.

"Suit yourself."

After two sandwiches, a long draught from the water jar, and picking and brushing the crumbs from his paisley vest, Helsby grew quiet. John jotted notes for a new composition. Helsby swayed. After the second time Helsby's head jerked, Helsby laid back, tented the newspaper over his face, and fell asleep.

He awakened as the train pulled into its destination.

"Johnny!"

John turned to his uncle's voice and pushed through the crowds to reach it, with Helsby panting behind him. Uncle Ralph shook John's hand and slapped his shoulder, and John let him, but the greeting felt stiff and unnatural coming from an uncle not exuberant by nature. Then Uncle Ralph noticed Helsby standing behind him.

"Your tutor?"

Helsby transferred his parcels to his left hand and extended his right one. "Andrew Helsby, sir, at your service."

"A pleasure, Andrew." To John, Uncle Ralph added, "Is your mother improving?"

The facts clamored for release. How John wished to say, "No, my mother is mad. Her mind shall never be sound again." He saw the open hopefulness on his uncle's face and wondered if his father hadn't performed an actual kindness.

"Yes," John lied. "She sends her best and plans to visit soon."

"Wonderful news. They'll be glad to hear it."

Before John could squirm under this falsehood, Uncle Ralph added, "Let's find your bags. I expect dinner's nearly ready."

John bounded into the wagon after the suitcases, but Helsby hesitated. Carefully, Helsby unfolded The New York Gazette and lay the pages on the boards before climbing in and perching on the edge of the seat.

As the wagon started on its way, Helsby gave John a nudge. "You're not afraid of soiling your clothes?"

John shrugged. "What does it matter? I rarely wear them twice."

The trip to Spencer Inn was a silent one. Uncle Ralph managed the reins and sank into distant thoughts. Helsby attempted light conversation, but when John didn't reply, he contented himself by pretending to enjoy the view, but his fingers spoke the truth by intensifying their grip on the crude seat at every jolt and bump. For John, the experience felt far different. The meadows of sweet blooming cordgrass; the venerable oaks out yonder; the clumps of bracken; the occasional marsh; and the rocking of the open wagon under a torpid, afternoon sky: these all worked in unison to unravel the snarled mass of Manhattan impressions and replace them with clarity and serenity. He had stayed away too long.

Uncle Ralph pulled into the courtyard, scattering the chickens, which voiced their protests with vigorous wing flapping and indignant squawking. He stopped the cart and began unhitching the horses. The backdoor flung open, and Auntie Eleanor, now also dressed in black crepe, rushed into the yard with exaggerated happiness.

"Johnny!"

She flung her arms about his neck and kissed his forehead.

"My, how you've grown! They must be feeding you well in New York. Oh, and you," Auntie Eleanor offered her hand to Helsby, who stood behind John, shuffling his feet. "You must be John's tutor. I'm Eleanor Wilson, one of Johnny's aunties."

Helsby let the parcels drop in favor of a hearty handshake and even heartier, "Pleased to meet you, ma'am." Then Auntie Eleanor tucked John's arm into hers and led him back to the inn. Helsby recollected his bundles and stumbled behind them.

"We planned a wonderful welcome home dinner for you, all your favorites," Auntie Eleanor rambled. "I declare Auntie Martha is making a slave of herself in the kitchen. She even made ice cream." She looked back at Helsby. "I hope you don't mind sharing a room with John. We're completely filled, even doubled up in some of the rooms. The latecomers are using the stables."

Before Helsby could answer, Auntie Eleanor opened the back door, releasing an enticing aroma of summer savory, marjoram, and thyme. Auntie Martha was pulling a chicken pie from the oven of the oversized cooker, and a patient blackberry crumble sat waiting to take its place, but she acknowledged John with a cordial nod before shutting the oven door and setting the dish on the windowsill to cool. Despite its abundance of guests, Spencer Inn felt as still as a forgotten cemetery; the

36

kitchen lacked bustling and laughter. Reality hit John like a brick in the face.

"Where is she?"

Auntie Eleanor's forced smile vanished. She and Auntie Martha exchanged glances.

"In the parlor," Auntie Eleanor said, "But..."

John headed for the doorway, but Auntie Eleanor was faster and blocked his passage.

"Johnny, this is all new for you. Don't you think..."

"Step aside, or I'll push you aside."

Auntie Eleanor's eyes widened. Auntie Martha gasped. But Auntie Eleanor stepped aside.

Even before John reached the parlor, he smelled the flowers: trillium, columbine, corydalis, and trumpet honeysuckle. He pushed the heavy door open and peered into the shrouded room, cold as a winter morning after the fire had gone out, and stinking of bad meat and perfume. Granny Spencer's beeswax candles blinked at his intrusion. Barrels of ice stood guard like evil henchmen. Mama Prudie's best ivory damask tablecloth didn't hide the cooling board balancing the homemade coffin. Sitting on a stool at the foot of the casket and resting his head against its edge was Papa Everett, cane lying beside him like a loyal hound. At the creak of the heavy door hinges, Papa Everett lifted his head, held out his hand, and smiled weakly.

"Come, Johnny, and see. No more cooking for fifty guests, scrubbing bed linens, and beating dust from carpets. She has her rest at last, and, I daresay, it's well-deserved."

John had never gazed upon a dead body, not even an animal one, and he did not know what to expect. Slowly, he inched toward the other end of the parlor, hesitated, and then peered inside.

In a box crafted by his grandfather and lined with the same crepe his aunties were wearing, lay Mama Prudie in her Sunday print dress, rigid arms crossed over her abdomen, stiff fingers clasped, eyes closed, mouth parted. This was not the cheery grandmother who whisked about the inn, forever cooking, baking, cleaning, or tending to someone's needs. Mama Prudie never lay this still, even in sleep. The soul sparking those once supple limbs had departed for heaven, wherever that was. What remained was nothing John knew as grandmother.

"I'm going upstairs to wash," John said. "Dinner will soon be served."

Helsby was already there, standing over the washbowl and drying his face. His frock coat hung from a nearby hook, which was why John noticed the holster on Helsby's hip.

With a sardonic chuckle, John shut the door. "Nervous, Helsby?"

"Not at all. Merely a precaution." He hung the towel and began retying the white scarf around his neck. "Come to Queens someday. You'll understand."

John hung his coat next to Helsby's, rolled up his sleeves, and reached for the lye soap. "I should think the gun would be more useful there."

"Mums has one. So does Tommy. And they both know how to use them."

Despite the lively gossip floating around him, John still sensed the eerie quietude. He tried to cover it by listening to the conversation and enjoying the meal, but everything tasted bland, and John spent more time pushing it around his plate than sampling any of it.

"Bad luck at the gaming table last week, I'm afraid..."

"Have you seen the latest pattern in Godey's? Scandalous!"

"Mrs. Wilson, what marvelous soup. Have you anymore?"

The entire scene felt wrong without Mama Prudie filling and refilling Spode China blue flowered plates and cups, babbling like a brook all the while.

"...isn't that right, Johnny?" Auntie Eleanor asked.

"Yes, ma'am."

"The chicken is first rate! Why, Why, Master John, you've scarcely touched yours!"

"Not hungry."

After dinner and an uninspiring scripture passage about the building of Solomon's temple, the guests drifted away to their respective rooms. John remained at the table, staring unseeing at the damask tablecloth. The evening felt flat and prolonged without the habitual piano concert, but since the piano resided in the parlor...

"I'm going for a walk," John abruptly said to Helsby, who lingered over one last cup of Spencer Inn's orange-spiced tea.

Helsby set the cup, still half full, on its saucer. "I shall accompany you."

They wandered into the yard, past the outbuildings and vegetable gardens and into the woods. Although just twilight, the compact trees shrouded the light and intensified the gloom John could not shake.

"Your family is perfectly divine. So is this inn...and the food! I can't recall the last time I supped so well. How do you leave such paradise?"

John snapped off a low-hanging branch and dragged it through the weeds. "Connecticut is a passing amusement, nothing more."

"Well, Master John, perhaps growing up with such delights makes you numb to them."

"You need to get out more, Helsby."

They ventured farther into the woods, the hushed night broken only by the occasional crack of a twig underfoot. As night deepened, an orange moon ascended into the velvet sky and lit their way. An owl hooted; an evil scream answered, and a skeleton with long white hair pranced across the path and disappeared in the brush.

Helsby stopped short and clutched John's arm. "What the hell was that?"

"My Granny Spencer."

"Your...granny...but..." Helsby shook from head to foot. "I thought, er, well, the funeral..."

"Mama Prudie is my mother's mother. Granny Spencer is my grandfather's mother. She lives in a cabin around here." John leered at Helsby. "Jars your sense of paradise, doesn't she?"

Helsby shuddered. "Merely fatigued by our trip. I'm walking back."

Suddenly, John felt as exhausted as Helsby claimed. "So am I."

"Really?"

"Yes."

Inside, John led the way through the dark building and up the darker staircase with Helsby close behind him, carrying a candle. The moonlit sky scattered phantom shadows across the floor, which did nothing for Helsby's nerves.

John laughed softly. "Helsby, you are such a girl."

But John banished the specters by untying the heavy curtains and lighting the kerosene lamp. Then John drew back the quilt covering the old bed, averting his eyes from his mother's needlework, but the image of her forming each patient stitch caused a lump to grow in his throat. Helsby settled himself on old wooden trunk at the bottom of the bed and began cleaning the pepperbox. John pulled aside a curtain and glanced at the window. His star winked back.

"I'm taking a bath." John let the curtain drop. "Shoot anything that moves."

The lump felt larger the next day, but John kept forcing it down. He never blubbered like a baby, not even during his father's most brutal whippings, and a female's death would not cause him to do so now. The parlor was filled with the guests fortunate enough to have either room or stable; the rest had bunked in their carriages or driven in that morning from town. Auntie Martha sat in the back bent over her devotional, the long veil framing her still pretty face, her lips moving in hushed prayers.

Papa Everett hunched on a chair near the front, leaned on his cane, and stared ahead, his eyes mournful. What a fool John had been to think his gregarious grandfather had set the merry tone for Spencer Inn. It was plain the inn's source of abundant life had taken her last breath.

During the entire affair, Papa Everett spoke but once.

"I thought for sure Christine would come.".

In a flash, Auntie Eleanor was kneeling by his side and patting his hand. "Christine would be here if it was possible. You know it's true, Papa."

"Who's Christine?" Helsby whispered.

"I don't know," John replied.

The room's stench was overpowering. Didn't anyone else feel nauseous?

"Friend of your grandmother's, perhaps?"

John swallowed hard, but his stomach quaked beneath his tight throat.

"I said, 'I don't know.'"

John slumped through the service as the minister opined about Mama Prudie. He trudged with the others to the village graveyard near the inn and then trudged back with the rest. He drooped through the post-service agape meal.

As the party dispersed, Uncle Ralph approached John. "Come ride with me."

Neither spoke as they saddled the horses and galloped away from Spencer Inn. They stayed out for the rest of the afternoon, each alone in his reflections, never breaking the silence until they returned to the horses to the barn and began feeding the stock their dinner.

Without warning, Uncle Ralph said, "I see you've noticed your Auntie Martha is not right in the head."

Astounded his uncle had mentioned what John never questioned, he pitched another load of hay. "Has she always acted this way?"

Uncle Ralph shook his head. "She was engaged. Once."

"A jilting?"

He again shook his head. "Name was Wyndham Franklin. Raised Morgans. One threw him the night before his wedding. He only lingered half a week."

John trembled, and he didn't know why.

"I'm sorry," he said.

John pitched another load. Uncle Ralph watched.

"You're slow, Johnny."

"A little sore." An understatement. He ached everywhere. "Out of practice, I guess." He paused, leaning on the pitchfork, and decided to go all the way. "Who's Christine?"

"Another auntie."

"Your sister?"

"No. She's your mother's youngest sister."

John blinked, and the lump grew larger. "My mother has never mentioned her."

"Can't say I'm surprised."

40

"Did she die?"

"No."

"Then, what?"

Uncle Ralph ripped open another bag of oats and shook them into the trough. "We don't know. One night, we had a late arrival, a regular swell, he was. Christine seemed quite taken with him. In the morning, both were gone. No one has seen or heard from her since."

"How long?"

Uncle Ralph removed his cap and scratched. "'Bout near a dozen years, I do believe."

Auntie Eleanor appeared in the doorway. "Dinner is ready."

After another meal John pushed around his plate, Auntie Eleanor shocked John by saying, "Let's go to the parlor. Johnny can entertain us."

Beaming, Helsby raised his teacup. "A veritable treat, I must say."

As family and guests filed into the parlor, John hung back. Uncle Ralph looked quizzically at John.

"I can't," John said in a low voice.

"Make a small effort. You needn't play long."

John turned to him in disbelief, but Uncle Ralph remained firm. "They require it tonight."

But even at the piano, John's muse was slow to awaken. His hands felt like heavy boulders. Any melody attempting to fly was hushed by Maestro's instructions, replaying in his mind like a nagging farmwife. After thirty minutes, John shut the lid and went upstairs.

He was climbing into bed when Helsby burst through the door.

"Master John, I had no idea you could play so well. Your father must be very proud."

"Yeah." John crawled under the quilt and pulled it past his neck.

"I don't mean to pry, and I certainly don't want to sound ungrateful for the post, but why aren't you attending prep school at Wesley Music Conservatory? It's produced many of this country's musical greats, including..."

"Because acceptance is via audition. Because it's nearly impossible to effect one without solid connections."

"But your abilities..."

"Then there's the matter of tuition."

"I'm certain Mr. Simons is well able to pay for it."

"He can. He won't."

"Ah."

John awakened the next morning to Helsby shaking him. Despite the warmth of the day, John shivered as he dressed. At breakfast, he picked at Papa Everett's sausage and Auntie Martha's mediocre attempts at Mama Prudie's flannel cakes.

"Leave him be," Auntie Eleanor said to no one in particular, as she refilled coffee cups from the stainless steel pot. "John needs to grieve in his own way."

John dozed against Helsby's shoulder on the way to the train station. The blast of the whistle woke him with a jolt, surprised they were still sitting in the wagon. Uncle Ralph helped the tutor carry the bags on board.

"Take good care of him," Uncle Ralph said, with a worried glance at John, already curling up in the seat.

Helsby clasped Uncle Ralph's hand in a congenial farewell. "Not to worry. Thank you again for your hospitality."

"All aboard!" the conductor yelled.

"I should leave," Uncle Ralph's voice sounded faraway.

"Please express my sincere appreciation to your wife for the care package," Helsby added in the distance. "I'll think of Spencer Inn with every delectable bite."

The train whistle blew a long blast.

"It's time," Uncle Ralph said. "Good-bye, Johnny."

The words fluttered around John's head like moths around a kerosene lamp during a middle of the night trip to the outhouse. As John lumbered through the tall grass, the wick burned larger and brighter and hotter until it ruptured into high flames and shattered the glass through the sky. Riding their crest was Satan himself, hair swept off his forehead and tangled in his thick horns, gray-blond strands sticking to his unlined face. He reached out with one hand and grabbed John by the neck, dragging him into the inferno and clamping his other hand around John's testicles. John coughed; he choked; the swelling in his groin gasped for release...

"Master John! Master John!"

... and he drowned in a sea of bilious agony...

"Wake up, Master John! You're having a nightmare!"

The tutor's rough shaking of John's shoulder hauled the boy into hazy, sweating consciousness as he vomited into Helsby's lap.

The next week passed in a scorching, doubled over blur of vomit, lucid dreams, and ice packs propped against his neck and between his legs, as the strangulation in both fiercely competed against each other for victor. Somewhere in the fog, John turned fourteen; he heard a doctor say, Just a touch of mumps;" and an angel in the form of Lucetta replaced the hellish hallucinations and lay cold cloths on John's hot face and slipped spoonfuls of broth steeped with healing herbs between his chattering teeth.

"Shhhh..."

John opened his eyes, pounding heart still racing. Gently, his mother lifted the damp locks from his wet cheeks and stroked his face with the back of her hand. She eased back the bedclothes, stripped off the nightshirt, and replaced it with another, fresh and clean. Water from the bedside pitcher trickled into a glass; she placed it to his cracked and puffy lips; he struggled to swallow. Her slender hands fluffed the down pillows, and he sank against their billowy mounds as she draped the sheet around his waist. He placed a sticky hand on hers and touched flesh. The angel was real.

"Mamma..."

"Go to sleep, Johnny."

The next time John stirred, early dawn was lighting the sky; the swellings had receded to lower case decibels, and his skin felt moist and cool. Had his mother really visited him in his anguish? Had her senses returned? He must find out.

John crept out of bed and plodded on unsteady feet across the third floor east wing to her room. As John turned the door handle, he heard faint squeals from his father's chambers further down the hall. His hand froze and pulled back. He slunk on silent toes to the other end of the wing.

Quietly, John opened the door, and tiptoed to the curtained four poster in the center of the room. He paused, heart threatening to burst from his chest, and gazed at hidden movement before him.

John flung aside drapes.

Skeins of amber hair failed to cover the nakedness of the household's newest chambermaid as she, with great and rapid energy, bounced on his father's nether regions.

"Christ!" Abbot yelled and knocked the chambermaid to the floor.

Sprawled out and dazed, she brushed the hair from her face. Then she, too, saw John.

"Ayyyyyyyyyyyyyyyyyyy!"

She snatched the sheet and dashed from the room, tripping over the silk. Abbott leaped from the bed, seized his smoking jacket, and stumbled to the sidebar. Hands trembling, Abbot splashed wine into a goblet and onto the tray, knocked the drink down his throat, refilled his glass as well as its neighbor, and then carried both vessels back to John.

"Drink?"

John slapped it away, crystal shattering to shards.

CRACK!

John tumbled onto the bed and sprang up, patting the left side of his jaw where his father's fist had met it, but the room spun like his old top, and he fell back, dazed. Yet, despite the buzzing in his ears and the blaze of ice in his neck, John managed to sputter, "I'm...telling."

"Humph!" Abbott raised the goblet to his lips. "Maybe she already knows."

"Liar!"

Abbott shrugged, dropped onto the bedside chair, and took another swig. "Then tell her, and see for yourself."

John closed his eyes against betrayal and bile. The throbbing in his face he could bear, but not the shredding of his heart.

Bounce, bounce, bounce...

He gagged; his stomach heaved. John opened his eyes. His belly returned to uneasy, but manageable, queasiness.

Abbott swirled the glass and studied its remaining contents. "She's fortunate I haven't sent her packing to Spencer Inn." He finished off the drink and glanced at John.

"Oh stop the wounded puppy look. It doesn't become you," Abbott said irritably. "See it from my viewpoint. Your mother prefers to dwell in world no one can enter, not even I."

"Which excuses adultery."

"And I fear, my son, you possess the same insanity."

That remark was an electric shock to John's pride. He flinched, composed himself, and glared at his father with all the revulsion his weakened body could muster.

Abbott continued. "You scorn me because I'm grounded in money, but money is the only thing real."

John's replied with a greater narrowing of his eyes.

"You doubt me? You've held gold pieces. By turns, you can grasp them to your chest or release them to make great things happen in the world."

So that was it. His father had given his mother a choice: her poverty or his philandering. John recalled the beautiful shell pacing her floors most days and nights and realized inhabiting a room in Satan's abode came with a steep rent.

"Why chase shadowy dreams when you can strut in daylight, where real men walk and thrive?" Abbott smiled, a mean cynical smile, and shook his head. "But soft, I'm speaking to a mere boy, one who cannot comprehend the ways of real men."

John strained and pushed himself to a sitting position. He paused, teetering, and then struggled to his feet. In two unsteady steps, he was towering over his father. To John's delight and despite the pain, Abbott shrank back.

"More to the point," John said, "is that you, sir, are not man enough for her."

Abbott jumped up, yanked an enormous handful of John's hair, and pulled him close.

"If you don't control your obsession with music," Abbott seethed between clenched teeth. "You will destroy yourself and anything you choose to love."

44

John jerked away from his father's grasp and tottered back to his room, collapsing into a heap in the doorway. The private nurse his father had hired heard him when he hit the floor and scurried to help him back to bed.

By dawn the next morning, John was sitting at the drawing room piano and playing with a new fever, foregoing his own compositions for those Maestro preferred, and tackling his academic studies with submissive viciousness.

"Enough ditties," Maestro said the following week when he returned, tossing the ruler on top of the piano and his Inverness onto his Abbott's favorite chair. "This isn't kindergarten. I want real music."

Without complaint, John launched into a rendition of Franz Liszt`s "Grand Etude de Paganiniin E Major," banging the keys fury, even Maestro didn't interrupt with a verbal or physical retort. Later, Helsby noticed his distress.

"You appear out of sorts today, Master John." Helsby sat opposite, folded his hands on the table, and leaned forward with a sympathetic smile as John translated a Michel de Montaigne essay from the original French into his copy book. "Perhaps you'd like to confide in me. They say a trouble shared is a trouble..."

"Fuck off."

It continued this way for another month. John poured himself into his dream and ignored the pleasantries. His father desperately needed topping. John intended to satisfy it.

One afternoon, as John was completing his summary to a critique of *Gareth and Lynette,* he felt a blunt object dig into his ribs. The room, sunny and warm with a slight southern breeze, went cold.

"Get up," Helsby said quite close to John's ear.

John sat, stunned.

"Helsby, what are you...?"

"Quiet!" Helsby hissed and thrust harder. "We're going for a little ride. Act normally; don't make a sound; and no one will get hurt."

Dumbfounded and still too weak to object, John pulled himself up and plodded to the door. Helsby cradled John's waist with one arm and maintained his assault with the other.

"Look, Helsby, if you need money..."

"I said, 'No talking.'"

"You won't get away with...OW!"

They met no one in the hall or on the stairs, normal for this particular Tuesday. Since Abbott would be gone overnight, he had given many of the servants a holiday, leaving just enough to care for Lucetta, prepare the meals, and take any unexpected calls. Living in lower

Manhattan amongst murderers and thieves had benefited the recalcitrant tutor. Helsby knew how to plot.

Once outside, Helsby prodded John toward the waiting carriage as a second one stopped behind it. Lord Girard exited the moment John stepped up, so Helsby nudged John forward and tipped his hat.

"What's this?" Lord Girard said, looking bewildered.

"School outing," Helsby replied with a nervous laugh as he shoved John into the carriage, leaped inside, and slammed the door.

Reclining on the far end of the seat was Maestro Seymour Cassidy. He glanced at Helsby's hand with a mixture of shock and amusement.

"Gunpoint, Mr. Helsby?"

"You said unobtrusive. I couldn't think of anything else." Helsby returned the pepperbox to its holster. "You know he opposes everything." With a shaking hand, he moved aside the curtain. Lord Girard trotted up the stairs and rang the bell. "It almost worked, too," Helsby added glumly. "I shan't doubt that I'm sacked."

Maestro looked straight ahead. "Then take comfort in this. Farlow Abbott Simons is about to receive one hell of a surprise."

The abduction couldn't be about money, not with Seymour Cassidy involved. Of what possible advantage could this scheme be to him? At any rate, John didn't have long to find out. In less than an hour, the carriage slowed in front of an enormous gated mansion.

"We're here," Maestro said.

Visions of dungeons and starvation vanished. Captivity couldn't get sweeter than this. One by one, they exited the carriage, John gazing about him in wonderment. The pepperbox remained in its holster.

"No tricks," Helsby said. "Assuredly, you will regret it."

In unison they ascended the steps. Maestro rang the bell. A pretty maid about John's age opened the door. No butler? Maestro handed her a card, which the maid read with earnestness.

"Oh, yes," the maid said. "He's expecting you."

Awed and confused, John stepped through the door into the spacious foyer and gazed around at the cathedral ceilings and gold-plated trimmings. The home's opulence brought his father's dwelling to the level of Granny Spencer's hut. Clearly, this was no ordinary kidnapping.

"Where are we?"

"The home of Oliver Dorchester," Maestro said.

John raised a bewildered eyebrow.

"Current president of Wesley Music Conservatory. You have an audition."

Unexpected tears burned John's eyes, and he blinked them back as he tried to stammer out a response.

"Don't thank me," Maestro said. "Thank Mr. Helsby. He's the one who approached me and pleaded for my interference."

The maid reappeared.

"Mr. Dorchester will see you now. Please come this way."

She led them through a series of wide corridors to a great music room. The tutor started to follow Maestro inside, but John took hold of Helsby's sleeve and tugged back. His teacher stopped, surprised.

"Helsby," John said in a voice low with emotion. "You did this for me?"

The tutor's cheeks turned bright pink. With an exaggerated flourish of his hand, he spluttered, "A moment of womanly weakness, for which I'm much embarrassed."

Again, Helsby stepped forward, and, again, John held him back.

"Thank you," John said.

The room's vast proportions made its few inhabitants appear as ants. A large concert grand commanded the center of the room. Nearby, in an oversized chair, sat a well-dressed man, about forty, with clipped auburn hair and an extra large auburn mustache.

"Approach the piano," Maestro whispered.

The magnitude of the moment caused John to tremble, but he clenched his fists to squelch it. He now realized the genius behind the plans bringing him here today. The spontaneity of their actions meant John had little opportunity to feel nervous or over-think this first official demonstration of his skills. He could only obey...and play. John started toward the magnificent instrument when Maestro said, "Master John."

John stopped.

"Don't make me sorry for today."

"I won't, sir."

John took his seat, uttered a silent prayer, and launched into a Frederic Chopin's *Fantaisie in F minor.*

Forty-five minutes later, at the far end of the room, Helsby, one eye on Headmaster Dorchester, leaned close to Maestro and whispered, "He doesn't move. He doesn't react."

"All good signs."

"Explain yourself, sir."

"He's still listening."

And Maestro turned slightly to Helsby and smiled.

"Telegram, sir."

Maestro left the room with the headmaster's maid to attend to its contents, leaving Helsby to enjoy the rest of John's audition by himself. Despite a quaking belly, clammy palms, and breaths coming a bit too quickly, Helsby couldn't resist staring into the distance, jutting his chin, and grinning.

CHAPTER FOUR: MAID TO ORDER

"You fired Helsby!"

Abbott handed his cape and hat to Gibbs, who bowed and hastened away.

"That lower Manhattan scum ought to be thankful I didn't file kidnapping charges," Abbott said, as he trotted up the stairs, with John rushing behind him.

"He's caring for a sick mother and a little brother!"

"Then he should have valued his employment and heeded my orders," Abbott called back.

"But..."

Abbott reached the landing. He turned to face John, who collided into him.

"Cassidy, I can't touch, but by the time I'm through with Helsby, he'll be lucky to be shining shoes outside Delmonico's."

Abbott turned left to the east wing, where he kept a home office. Frustrated, John stormed up to the third floor and over to his mother's effluvious chambers. Lucetta sat at the south window, bent over a piece of needlework, golden hair hiding cheeks growing thinner by the day. Dim sunshine squeezed between the bryony vines strung across the windows, normal compared to the bryony growing in geometric patterns along the walls and choking off the rest of the greenery. A variety of potted plants, some seedlings, some in full bloom, graced every shelf, table, and sill. Yet, not a single blade of grass marred the Axminster carpets.

"Mamma."

In and out; in and out; in and out went the needle. Lucetta did not look up. "Yes, Johnny?"

She was herself today.

"He fired Helsby."

Lucetta set aside the cloth, stretched, and yawned. "Johnny, I'm so sorry."

To prove it, Lucetta held out her lace-covered arms. John flung himself into the embrace of the one person who could make all the bad in the world disappear. She still smelled of lemon balm and verbena, and he burrowed his face into the comforting, fragrance and clung to her waist while her languid fingers worked his tangled skeins. His last haircut was before Mama Prudie's funeral.

"It's unfair," John's muffled voice cried out at last. "Helsby didn't hurt anyone."

"He'll find another position."

"*He* promises to ruin his reputation."

"It's a big world. Your father doesn't rule most of it."

"Helsby doesn't live in most of it."

"He'll be fine. He did it to himself."

John raised his tear-streaked face. "Mamma, how can you say such things? The conservatory audition, he arranged it."

"I know. He and I discussed it before he approached Mr. Cassidy."

"You...knew?"

Lucetta looked at him with so much love in her face, John felt as if the mother of his boyhood had returned.

"You must take your music and go somewhere with it. Your talent is not meant to be confined to Connecticut and your father's drawing room parties. Be happy your father has agreed to pay the tuition."

"Mamma..."

"Johnny, Mr. Helsby knew he would need another student this fall. You didn't think he'd be attending classes with you, did you?"

John once again buried his face, this time to hide his foolishness from his mother. He never considered the price Helsby's heroism cost him. Lucetta laid her cheek upon his head.

"Johnny, go forth and meet your destiny," she murmured. "And leave Mr. Helsby to find his."

John sighed in despondent resignation. He didn't care to admit it, but his mother was right. Whether or not the scheme succeeded, Helsby must have known he'd be out of job, at least where John Simons was concerned. His tutor had chosen. Helsby must accept his consequences. John must not concern himself with it anymore

A snake came crawling, it bit a man.
Then Woden took nine glory-twigs,
Smote the serpent so that it flew into nine parts.
There apple brought this pass against poison,
That she nevermore would enter her house.

He glanced up at his mother. His movement stopped her tuneless crooning, but her glossy cornflower eyes beheld things he could not see. Why couldn't she stay normal? He slipped out of her arms, but hers still grasped the son no longer there. He slipped away, unnoticed, and left Lucetta to her Atlantis.

John found the remaining weeks hard to fill. New York and Connecticut each had a routine, and John spent most of his young life adhering to one of them. Now, without a father to oppose or Helsby and Maestro directing his minutes, John felt lost. For several years, John relished the hours he could play as he pleased, without the interfering Maestro directing his notes. Now, whenever he sat at the keyboard, every lesson he'd learnt under that masterful musician's ruler spoke to him and guided each finger stroke. Maestro wanted to leave a legacy. Well, he accomplished it. He glanced into the night sky. His star agreed.

Finally the day arrived when John and an assortment of trunks boarded a train to Concord. He anticipated a full two day's journey, unless striking railroad workers aimed violence upon this particular locomotive. Such an inconvenience seemed unlikely. Most of the rioting was in Pennsylvania.

The trip passed without event, and the stagecoach was waiting for him at the depot, as per his father's orders. Porters loaded John's trunks in seconds.

"Wesley Conservatory," John said, stepping up.

"Straight away, sir," the coachman said with a tip of his hat.

Before long, John was standing before his new home: three Georgian-style brick buildings, full of elaborate woodwork, tightly woven carpets, and hand-stenciled walls.

Like the other preparatory students, John had a private dormitory at Collicott Hall with basic provisions: a single bed, desk, chest of drawers, and potbelly stove. Because the school catered to the offspring of the very wealthy, Wesley Music Conservatory did provide laundry and cleaning services, along with fresh water for drinking and bathing and the frequent changing out of chamber pots. John unpacked, storing his mother's corked herbs in the bottom bureau drawer to prevent spoilage.

At fourteen, John was the youngest student to pass through the doors of Wesley Music Conservatory, but it didn't take long for him to establish his place with the top pupils, in performance and composition. In drive, he surpassed them all.

As the Lord God did before him, John labored most hours for six days of each week and rested on the seventh. Weekday mornings he spent at Aubrey Hall with general studies: Latin, geography, grammar and rhetoric, algebra and geometry. The conservatory reserved afternoons and evenings for endless music instruction at McKenzie Hall. Three times a day, while his comrades gathered in the large dining room back at Collicott, commenting on how the fish was rather dry today and the soup a little thin, and how a more succulent duck can be found at the Cameron Hotel, Johns shoveled forkful after forkful, manure for his muse and tinder for his furnace. At night, while the rest of the all-male musical cast visited pubs and discussed their latest achievements, John haunted McKenzie Hall and played through the witching hours, with music theory books his sole company.

Concord hadn't any Roman Catholic churches, so on Sundays John remained in his room, studying scripture, humming Latin hymns, and napping. He recalled the country meals his mother once cooked for him during Connecticut summers, imitated them on the potbelly, decided his concoctions fared better than the ones served in the great dining hall, and, over time, weaned off slop for the masses and cooked for himself. Even when John left to wander the streets and clear the dust, the music in his mind drove him back to McKenzie Hall, his star spurring him on.

One September afternoon, in year two of the four-year program, while John strolled from Aubrey to McKenzie, a courier dashed up to him.

"Are you John Simons, sir?" the lad asked.

"I am."

"Telegram, sir."

Had something happened to Lucetta? John snatched it from his hands, opened it, and read:

MAESTRO DEAD -(STOP)- FUNERAL THIS WEEKEND -(STOP)- COME HOME IF YOU CAN. - (STOP) - HELSBY

The courier shifted from one foot to another.

"Any reply, sir?"

John returned the message to its envelope. Another piece of his world, snuffed.

"Yes," John said. "Telegraph Mr. Andrew Helsby and assure him he can depend on me. Also, send word to Mr. Farrow Abbott Simons for passage funds."

The boy bowed and sped away. John continued to the practice hall, determined to maximize his efforts knowing he would be absent from lessons for a brief time. Despite his resolve, a few traitorous tears fell anyway, but these John swiped away while dedicating his current composition to Maestro.

He lingered, well past dinnertime, so as to not miss the telegram from home. When none came, John cursed Concord telegraph offices for not being as sophisticated as New York offices and stopped by Professor Hugh Blanchard's rooms before heading back to the dormitory.

Professor Blanchard was surprised to see him.

"I'm leaving before the week is up," John said. "Personal business. I'll need a list of assignments, so I don't lose ground."

For a moment, Professor Blanchard looked confused. Then a light appeared in his eyes. "I'd forgotten Cassidy apprenticed you."

John blinked hard. Apprentice?

Professor Blanchard leaned his head against the door jam. "The world has lost a great teacher and even greater performer. We'll be all the poorer for it, may be rest in peace." He patted John's shoulder. "Take all the time you need. I'll have that list for you in the morning."

No return telegram arrived from his father that day or the next. Feeling desperate, John even checked with the downtown office at closing time.

"Search again," John snapped at the clerk.

"Sir, I've gone over this place three times. There's no telegram. And there are no funds for you."

John slammed the door behind him. For a moment, he stood, eyes squeezed shut, fists clenched, breathing heavy, forcing down boiling rage. Then he punched the building and broke into a run, past the campus, until he reached the Merrimack River. He stripped to his drawers and swam out. The icy waters, despite the day's lingering high humidity of Indian summer, cooled the lava inside him. Fifteen minutes later, numb inside and out, John re-dressed and trudged back to school. He bathed his hand and sent a second telegram to Helsby expressing his regrets.

The following year, when Papa Everett sent word Granny Spencer had died, John ignored it. Twelve months later, when Papa Everett sent a message Auntie Martha had also died, John paid no attention. Unwavering concentration on the goal was all John required. He forged ahead.

On the eve of graduation, Professor Blanchard summoned John to his office and inquired into his future plans. When John informed him he was to become the junior partner of F.A. Simons and Company and use those connections to promote his music, Professor Blanchard looked grave.

"Have you considered teaching, passing your knowledge and talent to the next generation, as Maestro did for you?"

"My destiny is greatness. I'm not a circus trainer."

Professor Blanchard slumped in his chair and regarded John thoughtfully.

"As you've witnessed, John, even the finest musicians will pass, but..."

John leaned forward. "Pray continue this enlightening speech."

Professor Blanchard raised his eyebrows. "But when you invest in a person, it continues into perpetuity."

"False. Otherwise the world would teem with Seymour Cassidys."

"Consider it, John. Headmaster Dorchester is offering you a post as my assistant. It will mean promotions, financial security, and opportunities for further creative expression."

"No."

"The position won't remain open."

John stood.

"I'd rather die."

"John, please reconsider..."

John shut the door with a firm click and strode out of the building and toward McKenzie Hall.

Neither Abbott nor Lucetta attended the commencement ceremony, nor did he anticipate their presence. But at the reception, John heard a familiar voice ringing through the crowd, "Master John! Master John!"

John strained to catch a glimpse through the sea of black caps. He spotted him toward the back, jumping up and down and waving his hand.

"Helsby!"

He pushed through the crowd and greeted his former tutor with a crushing embrace.

"Good God, Helsby, you've shrunk," John said, marveling they now stood eye to eye.

Helsby held the hand of a woman, a pretty young thing with yellow locks and a happy blush on her cheeks. Helsby looked as pleased as she, pink-faced and beaming from ear to ear.

"Congratulate me, Master John! I'm to be married this summer."

"Married? Helsby, is she the one you....?"

"The very same. Felicity Joy Bartlett, if you please, sir, the future Mrs. Andrew Helsby. Felicity, this is Master John Simons, my favorite and most difficult pupil."

Felicity's smile as John's lips brushed her hand was both open and sincere. John never realized someone so pure of heart walked the earth. Certainly such a woman never passed through the doors of his father's home.

"I'm delighted to meet you, Master John," Felicity's voice rang as clear as a crystal bell. "Andrew speaks so highly of you."

"Likewise," John said, at loss for words before such an alluring creature. Maybe he should spend time frequenting lower Manhattan.

"Invitations go out next week, Master John. I implore you, no regrets this time."

"I'll be there, Helsby. I give my word."

The next day, John departed for New York. Torrential rains slowed their progress, so it was twilight seventy-two hours later by the time John arrived home. Gibbs met the young master at the door and stripped his wet outer garments, but John scarcely noticed, so taken was he by the young maid lighting the lamps.

"Who is she?" John asked, trying to sound casual.

Gibbs chuckled. "Why, Master John, that's my Nora, all grown up, she is."

"Nora?"

54

His eyes stalked Nora as she flitted from table to table, long legs moving with the grace of a dancer.

"Mine and Janie's daughter. Don't you remember?"

Nora reached the last lamp. Her black and white uniform flaunted her large bust, narrow waist, and wide hips. John shook his head to clear the image and forced his attention back to Gibbs. "Janie?"

"My wife. She's headed up the kitchen staff since your birth."

"Ah, Cook, yes, of course."

The matching cap atop Nora's dark curls was the ideal backdrop for the maid's long lashes, turned up nose, and high cheekbones. Nora's lips pursed in concentration, as she slid her hand down the chimney, gripped it, and twisted it back into place.

"I'll have your bags brought up straight away, sir. Have you eaten?"

With a flounce to her step, Nora left the room, taking John's passion with her.

"Master John?"

"Yes, have Cook, er, Janie, send something to my room."

At the top of the third floor, John hesitated and then headed to his own chambers. Lucetta was, most likely, already asleep, and, if not, he wouldn't spoil this rather pleasant homecoming with more heartbreak. He could deal with her psychosis tomorrow.

But on his way to Lucetta's chambers the next morning, John encountered Nora dusting each rung of the grand staircase with precision. The tip of her tongue rested on her upper lip as she cocked her head and inspected her work. John shifted his balance, and the floor squeaked. Nora looked up, saw him staring at her, and smiled.

John turned on his heel and retreated to his room.

It continued this way for the next week. It seemed whenever John was most unaware, Nora would appear, teasing him with her lively eyes and pouty smile. He still had not talked to Lucetta, and his avoidance of fulfilling his basic filial duties irked him. On this particular afternoon, after napping over the New York Gazette instead of inhabiting the drawing room, John decided to stop avoiding the inevitable.

"Mother," John said, pushing open her door and stopping, shocked at the abundance of greenery in her room. "I've...I've come home."

Lucetta, bryony vines wrapped around her limbs and flowers knotted throughout her hair, sat in the old rocker that once graced his nursery, crooning as she jutted back and forth.

"Mother?" John whispered.

Lucetta rocked faster, bunching the carpets and scraping the floor. A vise wrapped around John's chest, and his throat ached from the rush of emotion. He bolted from the room and smacked into Nora.

"Oh, sir, I'm so sorry, sir," Nora said, but the sparkle in her eyes told John she was anything but sorry.

Glancing around quickly, John grabbed a handful of hair and pulled her into a spacious linen closet, the repository of towels and sheets for the entire third floor. In a moment, she was bent over; in a second, he slid in, far easier than he expected. John realized his mistake and lost it, which elicited a snicker from Nora, obviously more experienced than he. Horrified, John fled to the drawing room, pounded his shame into a brisk sonata, and pondered his next move.

John waited until the accountants departed for the night before approaching his father, sitting like Vlad Tepes on his throne, eager to mete out impalements.

"You must terminate the Gibbs family immediately," John said.

"Why?" Abbott asked, as he peered through his reading spectacles at a report.

John straightened his shoulders. "Insubordination."

Without looking up, Abbott reached for an envelope and handed it to John. "You're leaving for New Haven at the beginning of next week."

"New Haven?" John asked, annoyed his father had dismissed his request. "Why?"

"Ever hear of Warren Holloway?"

"The robber baron for the New England railroads?"

"Yes. He retired a few years ago and in the vicinity of Spencer Inn."

"So?"

"So he caught a bad cold last winter, which he didn't survive. His widow has hired someone full-time, but he can't start until autumn. She needs help with the stock and grounds for the summer. Your grandfather inquired if you could go."

"And you said, 'Yes.'"

"When you return, I'll set you up in business."

"And if I don't comply?"

Abbot raised his eyes. "You'll no longer have a home here."

John stalked away. The sooner he frequented New York City's key spots, the sooner the world would wonder at the improvements taking shape at F.A. Simons & Company.

In that spirit, John saw the latest Harrigan and Hart Broadway musical, dined at Delmonico's for the first time since leaving for Wesley, visited the Cooper Union for the Advancement of Science and Art and found the music instructor already knew his name, checked out the new temperance fountain on the West side of Union Square the staff were discussing, and biked through Central Park, thinking, thinking, thinking.

By night, John filled the drawing room with his masterpieces.

56

On Friday evening, John attended the debutante ball for Emily King at the family's Fifth Avenue estate, an ostentatious event he intended to shun until he discovered its advantage to him.

With a nod to the butler, John headed toward the gentlemen's quarters where he divested himself of both overcoat and hat and then checked his appearance in the mirror. He was adjusting his gold cufflinks when he heard a voice, "My word, it's Mr. Simons' son."

John turned around. Another young man was tossing his coat to the valet, but managed to extend his hand to John, who reluctantly returned the greeting.

"Mortimer Rutherford," the man said with an offhand smile. The exaggerated cut of his waistcoat and tails gave this lanky figure an almost hourglass appearance. "I'm delighted to make the acquaintance of Maestro Cassidy's apprentice."

So it was true. The world considered him to be Maestro's successor.

"Likewise."

As they exited the apartment and started toward the great hall, Mortimer said, "Tell me, sir, do the stories lie about your leaning toward finance as a career?"

"What have you heard?"

"A little of this, a little of that. You know how people talk."

"They do indeed."

Mortimer stopped short. "Sir, I'm no harbinger of gossip. I've a personal interest in your talent. My family manufactures pianos."

"I'm not in the market for an instrument," John said, increasing his pace.

Mortimer trotted up beside him. "Mr. Simons, you misunderstood my intentions."

The ballroom loomed. John disappeared into the crowd, leaving Mortimer to prey on a less fortunate soul. With the rest of the guests, John endured the first waltz of the evening, the one between Emily and her father, Jacob King. He grunted at comments of her incomparable beauty and her magnificent gown, white and studded with diamonds, a near-match for the single white rose in her white hair. These features, combined with Emily's alabaster skin, the consequence of having an albino mother, along eyes as blue as a Navy admiral's coat, reminded John of a porcelain doll.

A young voice behind him said, "Mrs. Claridon claims Miss King's dress cost a thousand pounds."

Another feminine voice responded. "T'wouldn't doubt it was true."

John avoided the polite conversation associated with waltzes and cotillions as best he could, answering female chatter in the fewest possible words when unavoidable, unless the conversation turned to his musical abilities, as it did when John danced the last dance of the night with Miss Emily King.

She signaled her desire with a touch of the fan to her lips, the number of unfolded sticks revealing the great privilege, since it was now his duty to escort her to dinner at midnight.

"This is truly an honor," Emily said, as the waltz began, "to dance with New York's most eminent musician."

"Thank you."

"Why, if I'd had my way, Father would have foregone the orchestra and hired you."

"Had your way?"

"Indeed, sir."

John studied Emily's face. It appeared sincere, lacking the coquettishness he abhorred in other girls of high rank.

"I don't understand."

"I asked. He refused."

"Did he?"

"Father said your talents were untried in polite society."

His gloved fingers tightened around Emily's hand and waist, and she murmured against it. A movement of the drapery across the room caught John's attention. A second alabaster face vanished beneath its folds.

"Mr. Simons, I meant no insult. He merely wished you had experience."

John eased up on his hold, and the distress on her face fled. "Who's behind the curtain?"

Emily dropped her voice. "Agnes. She's wicked jealous of me tonight. As she's only thirteen, Father forbade her appearance. But she cried so much he allowed her to peep. Please don't tell."

"Her secret is safe with me." \

Although John kept the appearance of interest and attentiveness, his mind roamed back to his mission long before the white soup was served. One person after another pulled Emily into their conversations, and John found it easy to nod his head at the appropriate time while pondering the results of this past week. As he soaked up the compliments, he realized his societal position was secure; a summer in Connecticut shouldn't diminish it. Satisfied, John left before dessert. He'd eaten his fill of sweets.

On Saturday morning, John scorned all breakfast, save for coffee, and spent a productive morning at the drawing room grand. After resolving a stubborn spot in a new piece, John was ascending the staircase to second floor dining room for a well-deserved late lunch, when he heard wailing from the back of the house. He retraced his steps. The commotion came from outside. As he approached the servant's door, he saw his father, arms crossed and looking most severe. Stuart Gibbs, hands clasped, tears streaming down his face, knelt before him. Janie and Nora clutched each other and wailed. Several of the gardeners formed an enclave around the party.

"Mr. Simons, I assure you, I never..."

"Thief!!!"

"I'll admit anything if you'll give us a second chance!"

"Tell it to the authorities. They'll be here shortly."

"At least keep Janie and Nora. They're innocent!"\

"Shut up."

"We're innocent, I tell you, innocent! My God, have you any idea what happens to women in a workhouse?"

Nora's eyes met John's; her despairing tears begged for mercy and absolution. Impervious to her plight, John once again turned to the main staircase, hoping Janie had prepared a decent lunch before his father had discarded her.

Yet, as John partook of the steak and kidney pie and contemplated his sonata in progress, the image of the disgraced Nora kept breaking into his concentration and spoiling his meal. The parlor maid received what she deserved, yet sharp claws picked at his conscience, spoiling the serenity of the sunny afternoon. One good thing resulted, however, and in this John took immense satisfaction.

Nora wasn't laughing anymore.

CHAPTER FIVE: POST-GRADUATE STUDIES

John woke well before dawn. Quickly and quietly, he washed, dressed, and then strode to the kitchen for a quick breakfast of bread and milk while the coffee boiled before heading to the barn and hitching a horse.

As he rode out to the Widow Holloway's farm, last night's conversation with Papa Everett swathed him like early morning mist on the verdure, a filmy presence he could not shake.

It had started out as merely annoying. Over dinner, Papa had praised John to the inn's patrons for dedicating his summer to helping a neighbor while John scowled into his stewed beef.

"It's not that she can't afford the help, you understand," Papa Everett said. "But it's hard to get the experience and reliability she needs for just three short months, especially since the Holloways were newcomers to these parts."

"More coffee, Johnny?" Auntie Eleanor asked, moving from guest to guest with the pot.

"Sure." John held his cup out. "How new?"

"Just last fall. Apparently, they've always kept horses, even after Mr. Holloway retired, and they traveled, rather extensively, from what I hear, fitting as the two of them were well-educated, as well as well-off."

Everyone laughed, except John. One of the men leaned forward and said in a hoarse voice, "Oh, you're referring to the railroad mogul. I read in the papers he had moved to the country, but I had no idea they meant here."

The large woman sitting next to him gasped. "Heavens! What brought him to these parts?"

Uncle Ralph passed the plate of sourdough biscuits to John, who absently took one and passed it along.

"Can't really say," Papa Everett said. "But they bought Wyndham Franklin's old place, empty all these years, and fixed it up quite nicely, from what I heard."

A strangled moan erupted from Auntie Eleanor. All heads turned. She covered her mouth and dashed from the room before Uncle Ralph could stop her.

"Shame Mr. Holloway died so soon after settling in," Papa Everett continued serenely, as if the interruption hadn't occurred. "Doesn't seem quite right he didn't get the chance to enjoy his little slice of paradise."

Mr. Hoarse pushed aside his plate. "Strange the widow would need a new farm hand. What about the help when the old man was alive?"

"Well, there's the rub," Papa Everett said. "They had no previous help."

A gasp ran around the table. The large woman choked on her beef, and Mr. Hoarse patted her.

"No help!" the woman spluttered, after a couple of large gulps of air and a sip of water.

"Mr. Spencer, sir, I'm afraid I don't understand." This came from the elderly gentleman on John's left.

"I don't either," Papa Everett raised his tea cup to his lips. "Somehow, they did the work themselves. After Warren passed, she assumed all the chores, but, as you can imagine, the work became too much for her. I don't see how they kept the place up and took care of the stock by themselves for as long as they did. It's not like they couldn't afford to hire someone, or even, for that matter, several someones, but they were recluses, I hear."

The horse loped along at a steady pace. The black sky was gradually lightening. John vaguely recalled the old Franklin place from his childhood, although he hadn't known the owner or its history at the time. No, the unsettling feeling hadn't come until later, when he had wandered past the inn for a solitary post-dinner walk.

Although John had pretended to aimlessly amble, his feet knew where to take him. By and by, Granny Spencer's cabin came into view, appearing even more ominous in its barrenness. He skirted around the dwelling and into the garden, long ago choked off by weeds and bryony.

"For they shall soon be cut down like the grass, and wither as the green herb," Papa Everett's voice said behind him.

Whirling around, John saw his grandfather, white hair glowing silver under the moonlight. Papa Everett smiled weakly. "Psalm 37:2."

John turned back and kicked his way through the underbrush, his grandfather's plodding footsteps behind him.

"How did it happen?" John asked dully, more from curiosity than any sense of caring.

"Believe me. You don't want to know."

John stopped. The time was long overdue. He turned around.

"I absolutely do want to know. My granny was a wild animal in the woods; one auntie runs away and disappears; another lived half-dead before her death; and my mother is insane."

His grandfather looked away.

"So, Papa, how did it happen?"

Papa Everett limped ahead, looking to the left, to the right, and at the night sky before stopping with a little sigh.

"Johnny, the answer is less in how she died than in how she lived." Balancing himself on the cane, Papa Everett placed a gnarled hand on

John's shoulder and regarded him through the twilight. "You're no longer a boy. Perhaps you should hear the truth."

He eased himself onto a charter oak stump and invited John to take another.

"My parents," Papa Everett hesitated as he groped for the right words, "met in an unusual way."

In the distance, a pair of eyes glowed an evil green, a warning to leave the past in the past.

"My mother, and, by the way, her name was Corina, my mother is not from here."

"She's not from Connecticut?"

"She's not from America."

"Oh."

"She lived most of her young life in a remote English village, where, though the Witchcraft Act of 1735 had outlawed the execution of witches, pockets of places still practiced the old ways. Eventually, my mother was tried and sentenced."

John glanced around the forsaken garden. "Because she was misunderstood?"

Looking down, Papa Everett shook his head. "Because she had poisoned her entire family."

The owl hooted and flapped away.

"And did she?"

Papa Everett lifted his eyes.

"Yes," he murmured."All of them."

"She murdered each member of her family?"

Papa Everett gripped his cane tighter and sat straighter.

"No, Johnny. She murdered all of her families."

Granny had borne fifteen children and had buried eight, as well as four husbands...she lived in poverty and isolation...she had the cleanest abode...no scraps ever...everything went into the garden...

"I...I don't understand."

"Because I haven't finished my story. So my mother was to be burned at the stake for killing, over the years, three husbands and eight children."

"Papa! How did she elude the law for so long?"

"We're talking over seventy years ago. In those days, death was frequent and expected."

"Maybe she didn't..."

"Hard to explain away when the constable finds your husband quartered like a deer, and you sitting at the table feasting on his entrails.

62

John's hand flew to his mouth, and he closed his eyes.

"So," Papa Everett continued. "Some of the villagers take in the remaining six children..."

"Seven," John muttered behind his hand.

"Six," Papa Everett repeated irritably.

John removed his hand and opened his eyes. "Fifteen minus eight equals..."

"Anyway, Johnny, my father, Brinsley Spencer, was a new minister in town and had visited her cell during the trial. My mother was not always a wild crone running through these woods. She was slender, waif-like, with black hair hanging to her feet. My father was also slender and quite the attractive man, Greek countenance and mild-mannered in temperament, yet strong in moral character. As he tried to save her immortal soul with pleas for repentance, she wove a hypnotic tale of the sinister plot against her, spurred by jealousy of her healing powers. Thus, she reeled him in, thread by thread by thread."

John's heart beat fast, but he held Papa Everett's gaze.

"Yet, through it all," his grandfather continued. "Her grief was honest and deep. That's what ultimately convinced him."

"Wait," John held his hand up. "She did kill her family?"

Papa Everett nodded. A soft breeze blew through the tall grasses, whispering secrets from ancestral ghosts.

"And yet she mourned them? That's insane!"

Papa Everett smiled sadly.

"He freed her and, in doing so, became a wanted man, so they fled to this country. My birth was her last. She labored to no avail," Papa Everett stopped and nodded to Granny's abode, "right there, in that cabin. If my father hadn't intervened, we both would have perished."

"Intervened?"

"As my mother lay bleeding to death, she gave instructions for removing her womb, and then me."

"And...and, she survived?"

"Survived...and thrived. Together they built and ran this inn until my father's death, when I was fourteen. At that point, I assumed control."

"How? You were just a boy."

"I grew up fast. My father is buried here."

Hands trembling now, John clutched the stump and looked around.

"You mean, in this garden?"

Papa Everett pointed behind him, in front of him, and over here and there.

"I came out when I realized what she had done," he said. "And caught her just as she was burying a leg."

John's trembling became violent shaking.

"You know the fear a wild animal has when you trap it? She had that look, Johnny. She shrank back when she saw me, even though I had not yet taken aim." Papa Everett hung his head. "In the end, I couldn't do it. Beyond the terror in her eyes, I could see the adoration my father had for her. You see, that was his crime; it was all of their crimes. She killed each one for not bestowing the worship she felt was due her. My mother possessed an insatiable need for deification. When she received it, all went well in her world. For the sake of my father, and for the doting mother she could sometimes be, I spared her life. Instead, I condemned her to the old storage shed, with a warning: if she took one step out of these woods, I'd blow her head right off her neck."

"And she obeyed you?"

"She knew I'd do it."

John said nothing.

"I invented a story about my father leaving town. Of course, no one saw him again. Your Mama Prudie and her family were staying at the inn when it happened. As it became obvious my father was not returning, and mother was forever damaged in her sorrow, they offered us a home. I countered with an offer of my own. To give credit to the loving memory of the people who became my in-laws, they stayed."

In a flash, John saw Mama Prudie bustling about the inn: cooking, cleaning, catering. For a long time, neither spoke. Finally, Papa Everett bowed low and broke the silence.

"For God will bring every deed into judgment, with every secret thing, whether good or evil," he prayed. "Ecclesiastes 12:14."

Nothing again, except the rustle of leaves as they joined the grasses in song.

Papa Everett sighed. "May she rest in peace."

"Amen."

Papa Everett held out his hand. "Help me up."

They started for the inn, and a troubling silence followed them.

"Her madness, Johnny, had become more apparent through the years." Papa Everett stopped and looked long and hard at John. "You understand, don't you?"

John closed his eyes and saw the Elysian Fields his mother had recreated in her chambers, and the swirling of her fine garments as she twirled through them.

"In time," Papa Everett continued. "Pity softened my grief. Lucky for me, most of the world forgot she lived here."

John reopened his eyes. "So she died in the cabin, alone, abandoned, as she deserved?"

Papa Everett looked away. "No."

64

"Then, how?"

He glanced at John. "She stepped out of the woods."

The outline of buildings came into view. John slowed his pace. He couldn't avoid spending his summer as a chore boy, but he could delay it. The white farmhouse, trimmed in dark gray, looked fresh and inviting in the early morning light. The shutters were still closed, a sign the aged mistress of the farm, in the distance among the ancient sycamores, hadn't yet stirred. He rode straight to the barns. Despite their age, they, too, appeared sturdy and well maintained, almost as if recently built. John hitched the horse and went inside the first one, meandering through the large building, gazing from side to side at the sleek thoroughbreds. The condition of the barn: impeccable. How had a single, elderly woman managed it, and did the widow really require his services? Maybe, John thought hopefully, she had hired another, and John could return home to his music and his rightful position at F.A Simons and Company.

"Well, well, what a surprise."

John turned at the woman's voice and beheld, not a crone, but a slim woman in her late twenties. Her straw-colored hair was piled under a wide-brimmed straw hat, which perfectly matched her blouse and neatly fitting trousers. John knew forward-thinking women sometimes wore pants, but he never encountered one who did. He stared at her manly boots, caught himself, and looked up.

"I'm seeking the Widow Holloway."

The woman's hazel eyes twinkled with amusement. "That would be I." She held out her gloved hand. "Savannah Holloway. And you are?"

Dumbfounded at this twist, John haltingly returned the greeting.

"John Simons. I'm the summer help."

"Turn around."

"I'm sorry?"

Savannah put her hands on his shoulders. "I said, 'Turn.'"

An unusual command, but John nevertheless complied. When he again faced her, he tried levity, hoping it would quell his inner quaking.

"Do I pass?" To John's chagrin, his voice quavered as he uttered it.

"You're here to work?"

"To work," John set his jaw and met her eyes with determined, almost defiant in their boldness, eyes of his own. "And to learn."

Savannah raised her eyebrows, but she also smiled, a half-smile of surprise and intrigue. With one hand, she gently grasped his face and eased it from side to side, as she bit her lower lip and inspected his features.

"Yes, you'll do nicely." She reached into a pocket and removed a folded slip of paper. "Here are your chores. You may begin immediately. Let me walk you around and outline my expectations."

Savannah talked as she escorted John through barns. With pride, she showed off the many horses. While John noted the location of feed and tools, he wondered at something Savannah did not mention. Hanging from pegs inside each barn were full outfits, clothing for men, clothing for women.

"...and your meals are included. In fact, you may help yourself from the icebox whenever you're hungry. Any questions?"

"Just one."

"Well?"

"Why do you keep clothes in the barns?"

Savannah cocked her head. "I thought you had farm experience."

"I do."

"Year-round?"

"No."

"Well, if you had," Savannah moved to leave. "You'd understand that torrential storms, thunders and blizzards, blow up from nowhere."

"If you say so."

Uncle Ralph didn't keep full suits in the barns at Spencer Inn, and those barns were as far away from the main house as those at Savannah's. Nonplussed, Savannah looked over her shoulder and shrugged.

"As I said, you'll learn," she sneered.

Throughout the day, as John pitched clean hay into the stalls, fed and watered the horses, and brushed them to a high sheen, he thought about the snatches of information Papa Everett had shared last night about the Holloways and the reality of the widow herself. Had the two of them really overseen this entire farm, and how? John smiled ruefully and shook his head. What little he had seen of Savannah suggested this wildflower would not wilt in the noon-day heat.

He worked steadily, never breaking except for food, drink, and the outhouse. He had just finished feeding the horses their evening meal and was preparing for the return trip to Spencer Inn, when Savannah, dazzling in white linen, trimmed in tiny buttons and ruffles at the high collar and wrists, appeared in the doorway and announced dinner was served.

John almost dropped the saddle. "Dinner?"

"Of course. I don't want the responsibility of you fainting on the way home."

"I don't fai.."

"You may wash up in the kitchen."

66

John dropped the saddle and turned to the house. Savannah was gone. Wavering between annoyance at her condescension and curiosity at what sort of dinner she might have prepared, John dragged his weary self up the rear stairs into the kitchen, illuminated only by the twilight entering the large window. A neatly folded muslin rested near the pump; a jar of soft brown soap sat beside it. John splashed water over his face, and his muscles, unaccustomed to hard, day-long labor, resisted the effort. Just as painfully, John refolded the towel, uncertain if he should wait for Savannah or locate the dining room himself. He lingered, debating. When she did not appear, John headed in the most logical direction. He stepped through the doorway and abruptly stopped.

Amongst the covered dishes winked many candles flames: solitaries, in pairs, in casual groupings, and floating in dishes of water; China and silver gleamed in their glow. Face framed by a few rebel tendrils from her regal pompadour, Savannah sat at the head, caressing a glass of burgundy wine.

"Coming in?"

"I..uh..yes."

In two steps, John slid into the seat at her left. Savannah reached for the decanter and filled his glass.

"Take as much as you like," she said, gesturing at the table. "I've already eaten."

John filled his plate with chicken fricassee and dumplings. Savannah drank wine and watched each bite with dreamy eyes. She didn't speak, although she did refill his goblet several times. At loss for a topic, John looked at his plate and ate until he thought he might burst.

"Well," John said when the last jelly tart had been consumed, just as the large grandfather clock rang nine times. "If I'm to return early, I must go." He started to stand, but the room swayed, and he sat again, more tired than he realized and dreading the long journey to Spencer Inn. If only he'd slept more last night and drank less wine this night.

"Don't you want to know what he was like?"

"Who?"

"Warren. My husband."

Sleepiness and concern for the ride home vanished as John realized Savannah intended to prolong the evening. "Yes."

"Warren," and Savannah's face softened; her eyes brightened; and she grinned with girlish delight, "was the most amazing man in the world, full of knowledge, marvelously strategic, a cunning fox in a den of wolves."

She rambled on how her husband manipulated the inner workings of the railroad system to his financial advantage, while John admired her animation, made all the brighter each time she uttered, "Warren," and Savannah uttered it often.

"How did you meet him?"

"Ah, well..." Savannah leaned forward and motioned with her finger. As John moved in, she moved aside his hair and brought her lips to his ear. John drew away in shock.

"I don't believe it," he said.

"Believe it, or not, as you wish. It's still true."

"You met Mr. Holloway at a P.T. Barnum circus?"

Savannah tossed her head. Her hair tumbled down, and John watched it fall.

"Yes. Our first date was at the wedding of General Tom Thumb and Lavinia Warren at Grace Episcopal Church in New York City."

New York City, John thought, so close to home. He couldn't take his gaze off her.

With a rapturous smile, Savannah turned her face to the ceiling and closed her eyes. "I'll never forget it: Tuesday, February 10, 1863."

"Eighteen sixty-three!"

The smile faded. Savannah opened her eyes and looked at John. "Why does that shock you?"

John's face turned hot. "Because you don't seem to be..."

"We were married almost twenty years."

"I don't see how..."

"John, why don't you just ask? I don't mind telling. I'm thirty-seven."

Thirty-seven? Impossible!

"No...children?" John asked, trying to sound nonchalant and failing.

"We never wanted any. We had each other, you see, and the horses."

"But don't babies just...?"

"There are ways to prevent them." Savannah's voice was curt. "Anyway, it's late. You must go home."

"Home?"

John's heart sank. He had assumed that, since it was this late...

"Yes, home. I want you here before dawn."

The clock struck twelve. John didn't move. Savannah placed a hand on his.

"I changed my mind." Savannah squeezed his fingers. "I want you to stay the night."

There are ways to prevent them. And Savannah knew those ways. Before John could act on the joy leaping up everywhere, Savannah added, "You may sleep in the barn."

John woke the next morning to sunlight, pounding temples, and a jouncing in his middle that felt like motion sickness. Somewhere a horse nickered; the inaudible voice of Savannah responded. With a groan, John sat, brushed straw off his clothes, rose onto unsteady feet, and plodded to the adjacent stall, picking hay out of his hair as he went. Savannah was brushing one of the thoroughbreds.

"If you're going to work for me," Savannah said, not looking at him and still brushing, "I expect you to be on time."

His first day, and he'd already disappointed her.

"I understand," John said, understanding all too well.

"There's breakfast in the kitchen. Be quick about it. I don't want you fainting in my barns."

"I don't fai...never mind. I'm not hungry."

Savannah slid the brush into her back pocket. The horse whinnied and stamped a foot. Savannah shrugged and held out an apple.

"Suit yourself, John, but remember this." She glanced over her shoulder. "I don't offer twice."

Heart heavy, John trudged to the kitchen, ate very little of the porridge still left in the kettle, and quickly returned outside. Together, they worked, in silence, with Savannah's crisp voice intermittently breaking the quiet by announcing the next task. This surprised John, for he had assumed that, as the hired help, the farm duties belonged to him. When the sun stood straight in the sky, Savannah ordered him into the house, where John partook of last night's vegetable soup and the rest of the bread, before returning to his duties. About mid-afternoon, Savannah sent him to the Hopkins farm for milk and eggs. The sun was still shining when John turned to ask Savannah a question and realized she was nowhere in sight.

At dusk, John again climbed the rear steps to the farmhouse. The kitchen was empty and dark; no welcoming muslin or soap greeted him by the pump. He stepped into the dining room, also dark. No tea lights beckoned as they had last night. Dismayed and confused, John rode to Spencer Inn with only the moon and his star to guide him. As he wolfed the last of the baked beans and cornbread, Papa Everett tapped in.

"How's the job?"

"Fine.

He wearily climbed the service stairs to his bedroom.

As the days progressed, John's admiration and passion for Savannah grew faster than the corn in the distant fields. She was unlike any woman he had encountered in his young life. By day, Savannah, stunning in men's work clothes, consistently outshone him. She pitched hay faster than Uncle Ralph, nimbly swung an ax, and broke the wildest of horses. On the evenings Savannah chose to cook, she presided over the dining room table with the majesty of Helen of Troy and enthralled him with stories of her life with Warren...before banishing him to the barn.

After passing one such miserable night with the thoroughbreds, John had an idea. He entered the house while it was still dark, surprised that Savannah had left the rear door unlocked, and never noticing dawn had broken until Savannah's voice disrupted his thoughts.

"Oh, aren't you the honey!"

She stood in the doorway, wrapped in charcoal blue and barely pink; beige ruffles at the collar, shoulders, wrists, hem, and down the middle where two lucky ends of the dressing gown met. John flushed both at the sight and her delight, but he covered it by flipping another flannel cake and pouring steaming coffee into a gilded rosebud cup. Savannah brushed away her cascading hair and accepted the cup with one hand while yawning into the back of another.

"If you'd like to get dressed," John said, wishing she would not. "Breakfast is ready."

"What's the sense of a cold breakfast?" Savannah eased into a chair two hands around the cup as she blissfully sipped, while John, spellbound, drank in the image.

Savannah raised her eyebrows. "Well?"

So John served scrambled eggs, flannel cakes with maple syrup, toast and butter, and newly-made applesauce. While Savannah matched him bite for bite, she told John about hers and Warren's last trip to Europe.

"Davenport China," Savannah murmured, tracing the gold lines with a finger. "Did you know the Prince of Wales ordered it?"

"I did not," John rose. "More coffee?"

"Mmmm..." Savannah said, lost in reminiscing.

The grandfather clock in the next room chimed eight. Savannah's euphoria turned to disapproval.

"It's late." Her soft voice was edged with irritation. "Shouldn't you have started?"

Before John could answer, Savannah coldly added, "Wash up the dishes first."

It continued in that vein all week. Sometimes Savannah decided against John's bunking in the barn, and he'd plod to Spencer Inn, arriving long past Papa Everett's nightly concert. After gobbling leftovers and a quick sponge bath, John tumbled into bed. Papa could have all the performances. Between exhaustion and all-consuming contemplations of Savannah, taking the piano bench and entertaining the inn's patrons seemed like faraway memories.

On Friday afternoon, as John was brushing Bella, Savannah appeared out of nowhere. "Would you like to ride her?"

John glanced at the shiny brown coat. Bella was definitely a beauty.

70

"May I?"

"Of course. We've worked enough for today."

John's chest began pounding, and he was helpless to stop it. "We?"

"Yes, 'we.' Get Longfellow ready for me."

For two hours, they traversed the countryside, lush and green in its summer glory. They stopped to rest the horses near a brook and knelt beside babbling waters to cup their hands and drink. Face dripping, Savannah stretched out in the grass, flung her arms above her head, and blissfully contemplated the clear blue sky. John, suddenly shy at her unexpected childlike openness, sat beside her, hunching his knees.

Thinking he ought to speak, John said, "So you met Mr. Holloway at a circus?"

"That's correct." Savannah wriggled like a puppy and turned to look at him. "Why do you ask?"

"Just wondering what motivated both of you to attend a circus at the same time."

"I never said I attended the circus. I said I met him at the circus."

Curiosity replacing timidity, John lay beside her and propped his head with one hand. "Seems to me attending would be a requirement."

A sly look appeared in Savannah's eyes. "Not when one works for Mr. Barnum."

John blinked. "You worked for P.T. Barnum's circus?"

"I was a bareback lady."

"A bareback lady."

"Yes, on an elephant." Savannah laughed, a full, deep melodious laugh.

"You made that up!"

Savannah tweaked his cheek. "What if I did? You can neither prove nor disprove it."

"Seriously, Savannah," and John's voice caught. He had never spoken her first name aloud, and he still felt the prints of her fingers. "How did you meet Mr. Holloway?"

Smiling impishly, Savannah sat up and tossed her head. "I'll bet wild blackberries grow around here."

In a flash, she had crawled away on hands and knees to the bushes, with John automatically following her lead. They crept through the brambles, pushing them aside, and passing on the red berries in favor of ripe black ones. Next month, John promised himself, he'd surprise Savannah with a batch of Spencer Inn sumac lemonade.

"Ooooh, Johnny," Savannah cried, as she plucked a large berry. John's heart opened wide at hearing his childhood nickname with her voice. "Here's a juicy one for you." And she pressed the fruit between his lips.

Without thinking, he caught her fingers between his teeth and held them. Savannah raised her eyebrows at his audacity. John paused, allowing his gaze to settle on the twig twisted in her hair. He let the fingers go and inched his hand. Savannah's eyes followed the movement until he touched silken strands. As he unwound the twig, John bent close and tasted something sweeter than blackberries. She briefly parted her lips at the touch of his and pulled away.

"We need to go," Savannah said, the expression beneath her downcast lashes revealing uncharacteristic vulnerability. "Your grandfather will wonder."

John returned to Spencer Inn that night, ecstatic he had finally broken through Savannah's hard shell, but the next morning, she was as curt and businesslike as ever. The difference was that Savannah prepared dinner nearly every night and that the details she shared about her marriage with Warren grew more and more intimate, when Savannah cared to share them. On far too many nights, Savannah was content to sip wine and stare blankly into a candle flame, returning to reality only to remind John his haystack awaited. The last time it happened, John had overslept and bolted to his feet, fearful of Savannah's reprimand. But except for the whinnying of the hungry horses, the barns were silent. Ignoring Bella and Longfellow's demands for food, John had dashed into the house and found Savannah where he had left her the previous night, still awake, still riveted on the stump of a cold candle. Shaken, John had slipped outside and tended to the horses. Savannah did not appear until close to lunchtime, but she had remained withdrawn.

One muggy mid-July morning, John arrived at the farm in time to see Savannah, immaculate in her riding clothes, saddling up Longfellow.

"I'm meeting my accountant in New Haven," Savannah said. "I shan't be gone all day, noon, I would think."

"Yes, ma'am."

She galloped away. John stood, watching the proud figures until they vanished beyond the horizon line. Then, and only then, did he set out for the barns. The farm felt empty without Savannah. Thoughts of their time together displaced the music in his head, as he dutifully scrubbed compartments and replaced hay and fed and bathed the horses. Noon came and went. The air hung heavy and oppressive; the clouds darkened as the afternoon deepened, and tension mounted in his soul. By late afternoon, the distant rumbling had grown threatening. The horses shuffled restlessly in their stalls, and the quiet wildness in their eyes shone through the waning light. John was hanging the pitchfork near the entrance when a boom, a loud crack, and a blinding light made him jump just as the largest sycamore fell. When the scene cleared, there was Savannah, sitting motionless atop Longfellow. She neither spoke nor blinked. Then lightning spliced the sky and savage rain pelted forth. Longfellow bolted for the barn. Once inside, Savannah quickly dismounted; John grabbed the lead and started walking Longfellow to his chamber, as Savannah rapidly unbuttoned her shirt. John hypnotically watched each movement.

"Are you kidding me?" Savannah's voice rang out.

John hustled Longfellow to his stall and dashed back in time to see Savannah toss the shirt onto the ground.

"For God's sake, John!" Savannah kicked off her boots. "Why are you staring?"

"You're all wet."

She stepped out of her pants and began twisting water from her hair.

"Why, I suppose I am!" She reached for the clothes on the hook.

"Savannah, wait."

"Look, I'm neither a mawkish schoolgirl nor a country maiden. I thought you could handle that fact."

"I can."

In hindsight, John recalled only a blur, a holding of Savannah's face in his hands and forcefully kissing her, never slowing, never stopping until his initial violence had drained and the torrents had slowed to drizzles. Beside him, Savannah fidgeted, but John held her fast.

"Don't make me leave tonight," John whispered.

Savannah entwined her fingers in his hair, threw a strong leg over his waist, and scooted closer, ready for round two.

"I won't," she said.

John woke the next morning stiff, sore, and prickly from lying naked in straw all night. When he found Savannah in the bright and warm morning sunshine, dew glistening like wet diamonds on the grass, she was about to mount Longfellow. Boldly, John approached her and kissed the nape of her neck. Savannah did not respond.

"Your breakfast is waiting inside," Savannah said.

That's when John noticed the neatly stacked wood pile by the rear door. The sycamore was gone.

"You're leaving?"

"Only for the morning. I left early yesterday to beat the storm."

Savannah's coolness persisted for several days. On the evening of the third, she prepared a modest dinner, well, modest for Savannah: stewed rabbit and dumplings, French vegetable soup, Yorkshire biscuits, and something Savannah called "silver cake," rich in mace and citron. John quietly ate, and Savannah monitored the candle, until she abruptly asked, "Would you like to see the rest of the house?"

John immediately dropped his napkin.

"If you like," he said with a smile.

The oak floors, walls, and planed staircase played canvas to French brocade drapery and upholstery and unusual paintings and artifacts. For inside that farmhouse were Renaissance oils, Baroque sculptures, as well as a Tongan paddle club, a sixteenth century Turkish map, an Aztec calendar, a Dendera lamp, a Phaistos disc, a Germain Royal silver tureen, a Townsend Chippendale antique secretary, an eighteenth century oriental porcelain flask, a Pinner Qing Dynasty vase, an eleventh century Olyphant, and 1240 "Sifridus" chalice from Germany's Osnabrück Cathedral.

As Savannah pointed out each item, she told the story of how she and Warren acquired it, so that hours passed before they reached the drawing room, not so very large, but cozy, in its crackling fireplace, heavy bookshelves, and grand piano with beautiful swirls in its finish.

"I admire you," John said.

"For?"

"For staying here, alone, with your memories. It must be quite painful for you." His eyes strayed to the center of the room and stayed. "Do you play?"

"The piano? Oh, God, no!"

John's fingers crawled, and he clenched his fists to make them stop.

"But Warren played, and quite well, too." Savannah must have noticed his crestfallen expression, because she added in the next breath, "Don't tell me you play."

"I graduated in the spring from Wesley Music Conservatory."

She raised her eyebrows. "Really? Where Oliver Dorchester is headmaster?"

"The very same."

"Now that you mention it, I do recall hearing something about it." She tilted her head and smiled teasingly at him. "Well, Mr. Simons, let's see what you can do."

His fingers prickled again. "May I?"

"Of course."

John needed no further pressing. Quickly he sat, eyes passing over the beautiful wood.

"Isn't it gorgeous?" Savannah said. "Only burr walnut creates those marks."

"Burr walnut?"

"It's a Schwechten. Warren ordered it from Berlin." Savannah impatiently tossed her head. "Enough about the piano's origins. This isn't a history class. Play!"

74

John looked up, but Savannah's mouth was full of mirth. He played, and as he played, Savannah leaned over the piano, wine glass in hand, and her mind, well, who knew where that traveled. Near the end of the third song, John stole another peek. The mist in Savannah's eyes...God, she was beautiful. He stopped playing, pulled her tight, and tasted salt.

"You're right." Savannah glanced away. "I shouldn't be alone. Far too many memories."

John gently grasped her cheeks and made her face him. He kissed her again. "Then let's make new ones."

Before Savannah could object, John swept her in his arms and carried her upstairs.

He awakened the next morning before she did, in humbled disbelief at finding himself there, awed beyond words that she had allowed him to remain all night in her bed, the bed she probably had once shared with Warren. The room, although small, seemed spacious, due to its sparse furniture and white lace fluttering at the wide-open windows.

The bedclothes rustled. Savannah stirred, stretched, and smiled up at him. "You're late. The stock is probably..."

"Savannah, will you marry me?"

"Marry you! Goodness, John, you're a mere..."

"I'm serious. Will you marry me?"

At the earnestness in his voice, her expression turned to steely determination.

"I shall," Savannah lifted her chin. "Yes, John, I will."

John kissed her long and hard. A loud bray, and he remembered the hungry horses. Reluctantly, he reached for his breeches. Savannah leaned against the mound of ruffled pillows, looking thoughtful.

"John, don't announce it yet."

"Why would I wait? I want to share our good news with the world."

"Because it's sudden. It will come as a shock, to some. Let's share it by and by."

John stood and hitched up his pants. "One person must know immediately."

Savannah raised her eyebrows and looked almost alarmed. "Who? Your grandfather?"

"Andrew Helsby."

"I beg your pardon?"

John slid an arm into his shirt. "My former tutor. His wedding is this weekend. You'll go, of course."

"Well, of course."

"Helsby will surely guess it when he sees you on my arm. For reasons you do not understand, I want Helsby to know."

The playful smile returned. Savannah climbed to her knees and threw her arms around John's neck.

"Then Mr. Helsby should know at once." Savannah tossed her head. She looked young and happy and that warmed John inside and out, for he caused the change. "Mrs. John Simons. I can't wait!"

John kissed her again, easing her onto the bed, until he again remembered the stock. He pulled away and reached for his boots.

"Savannah, I'd like to go into New Haven this morning after I feed the horses."

"New Haven? Why?"

"To telegraph Helsby."

"Oh, yes, of course."

Once again, Savannah appeared subdued, but John shrugged it away and hurried to the barns. Halfway through the morning chores, Savannah joined him.

"I had to make arrangements for the horses while we're gone," Savannah said.

Several hours later, John was standing in the New Haven telegraph office, informing Helsby he was bringing a surprise guest to the wedding. John waited for the response, which wasn't long in coming. Helsby soon telegraphed his congratulations.

All that week, John did not return to Spencer Inn. Each morning when John opened his eyes and found himself still lying in Savannah's bed and gazing at the beauty curled against him, he lifted his soul heavenward in perfect thanksgiving, his heart too full of emotion for words. All dreams of performance fame had vanished, and he no longer needed F.A. Simons and Company. Savannahs' wealth would be sufficient. Every evening, they inhabited the drawing room, with Savannah riding on the crest of memory and old imported wine, while John played the song he worked out mentally for her all summer and soared on the growing fancy that all his compositions would now be for her.

"How marvelous that my house should be filled with music again," Savannah murmured.

Then a shadow crossed her face, and she said no more.

On the day before the betrothed were to depart for New York, John trotted to Spencer Inn to pack his trunks for the final time. After Helsby's wedding, he would send to New York for the rest of his possessions. As he fastened the smallest suitcase, John heard the floor creak. He glanced up. Papa Everett stood in the doorway, gripping his cane.

"That's quite a lot of clothing for a short trip, Johnny."

76

"I'm not returning to the inn."

"Well." Papa Everett limped into the room and leaned on his cane. "I'm sure with the distance between the two farms, it's easier to stay on site."

"It is."

And John left to find Uncle Ralph.

Not once during the journey to the Holloway farm did Uncle Ralph speak, not did John expect anything but silence from Uncle Ralph. He did appear a little surprised at John's request for a ride and even more surprised when John loaded his entire luggage into the cart. But Uncle Ralph remained true to himself. He did not ask. Auntie Eleanor was busy in another part of the inn and didn't know John was leaving for good. John didn't care. Uncle Ralph could tell her.

At the farmhouse, Uncle Ralph helped John unload the trunks.

"Thank you," John said.

"You're welcome."

Ralph climbed onto the cart and drove away.

The grounds were deserted; the barns were empty except for the horses. Wherever could Savannah have gone? John brought the trunks into the house and up to the second floor. No Savannah anywhere. Her office, perhaps?

In their bedroom, he saw the sheet of paper pinned to the pillow.

I have a financial problem that requires immediate attention. I'm staying in New Haven overnight. I shall meet you at the train station.

The lack of signature unsettled him, but, then, he rationalized, why would Savannah sign it? No one else lived at the farmhouse. The barns felt empty without her, and John plodded through the chores they had performed together all summer. He picked through the ice box once or twice and went to sleep early, the large bed feeling gargantuan without her presence. John's spirits rose the next morning, and they continued to rise as he and the luggage settled into the Hansom cab. He pictured Savannah waiting at the depot, poised, but quivering inside with comparable excitement.

Peering through the crowds of morning travelers at the train station, John's heart rapidly sank. He inquired inside and learned Savannah had cancelled her ticket. Before John could react, the clerk pushed a folded piece of paper under the glass.

"She left this for you," the clerk said.

John snatched it and read:

I have business on the farm that needs attending. I am unable to accompany you. Regrets.

Again, Savannah had added no signature, no fond terms of endearment, nothing. The train whistle blasted a loud warning. John couldn't miss Helsby's wedding; he had given his word. With a leaden heart, he hurried to boarding. It was a bleak ride to New York.

Helsby, with Felicity happily clinging to his arm, was waiting for him when the train pulled into the station. After crushing his ribs with an enthusiastic embrace, Helsby looked around. "Why, where is your guest?"

"She had a scheduling conflict."

"Ah."

"Be assured, Helsby, you shall meet her very soon."

"I shan't rest until it happens." Helsby started to take the suitcase, but John moved it away.

"It's a several-block walk, Master John."

"Believe me, Helsby, this is nothing compared to my servitude this past summer."

"My condolences." Helsby eased Felicity through the crowds, with John beside him.

"Save them, Helsby. I never would have met 'her' without it."

Helsby covered a knowing grin by saying, "Tommy arrived last night. The charity school granted him a holiday, one of the perks, I suppose for my overseeing operations at an industrial school."

"Headmaster, again?"

"Yes. Not quite to my liking, but steadier than tutoring, now that I'm to be a family man."

"And your mother? Will I meet her, too?

"Unable to attend, I'm afraid."

"Because she went home to Rhode Island?"

Helsby stopped and regarded John with soft eyes.

"She did make it home, but not to Rhode Island. She's passed onto her eternal home, Master John, one without sorrow or pain, and I, for one, am glad."

"I'm sorry, Helsby."

"She suffered much, Master John, more than any good woman should."

As they moved away from the station, the streets grew filthier, the people shabbier, and the houses more tired and dilapidated than anything John had seen near the depot. Lower Manhattan hinted at none of Upper Manhattan's splendor, only cracked windows, sagging roofs, and residents moving with weary hopelessness. Groups of scowling men slouched against buildings, hands in pockets, and staring into the street made John feel very glad for Helsby's pepperbox. As they gradually moved into the business district, the buildings looked less desperate; the bustling foot traffic moved with brisk steps; and modest carriages rolled along the streets, spewing dust and debris as they went. Helsby's apartment was above a sausage shop, next door to Hewes Music Hall.

"Dana Hewes is the owner, English, and a most enterprising man," Helsby said, opening the side door. "His establishment is always full."

The stairs creaked and smelled of mildew and stale cigarettes. At the third floor, Helsby led them through a narrow hall of densely packed doors, stopped at one, and unlocked it.

"Well," he said, gesturing for Felicity and John to enter before him. "I present Villa Helsby."

A small foyer led directly to a small dining room, the center of the apartment. Before John could react, Felicity removed her bonnet, said, "Excuse me. I must freshen up, or I'll be late," and disappeared into the cubicle on her right. Directly opposite was a water closet.

"Plenty of windows equal plenty of natural light," Helsby said. "Saves on kerosene."

John followed his gaze beyond the dining room and onto the fire escape, where rows of clothing were strung across the platform. A naked child stood sucking his thumb and clutching his mother's apron as she hung another tattered shirt. A second boy, barefoot, his trousers rolled to the knees, sat on the slats, whittling. Three urchins, in greasy suits and caps, huddled near the wall and against each other, sound asleep.

"Of course," Helsby added. "The view is less than desirable, but one cannot have everything."

"I understand."

From the dining room, John could glimpse into the rooms on his left. Behind him, a scullery, beyond him, the parlor. The door at his right remained closed.

"Master John, I do appreciate your delicacy. Some might feel mine and Felicity's living arrangements are most improper, but necessity spurred them, you see."

"Necessity? Helsby, is she...?"

Helsby turned crimson.

"Master John, I assure you, the future Mrs. Helsby's honor is quite intact." Helsby dropped his voice. "She'd been keeping house for her widower father until, well..."

Here, Helsby's voice became a whisper, "...until her father died. We don't speak of it as it makes her cry. But she couldn't very well stay there alone."

"You don't have to explain."

"So I left the boarding house and rented this flat."

"I would never judge you, Helsby."

"Convenient, too. I can walk to school. Saves the cost of transport."

The other bedroom door opened and an unsmiling young man, about fifteen, entered the room, carrying a book. He'd parted his well-greased curls severely to the right and wore a suit that was a little high in the ankles and a little short near the wrists. But the fabric was neatly brushed, the high collar crisply pressed; and the bow tie flat and perfectly knotted.

"Master John, my younger brother: Mr. Thomas Helsby."

The boy transferred the book to his left hand and held out his right. "Your servant, sir."

"Master John is here for the wedding." Helsby turned to John. "Where might you be lodging?"

"We were to stay at Sturtevant House..."

John stopped, the image of the squelched fantasy weekend too painful to contemplate.

"I know it's cramped, and not suitable to your position, but in light of your altered plans, would you consider...?"

"Helsby, I'd be honored."

"It'll be three to a room."

John thought of the many nights he'd slept in Savannah's barns. "It's one night. Where is the wedding?"

"The Methodist Episcopal Church down the street."

Felicity reappeared wearing a deep peach afternoon dress and white gloves and bonnet. Thomas disappeared into the bedroom.

"I'm ready, Mr. Helsby," Felicity said, cheeks rosy with anticipation.

Helsby looked at John.

"The ladies of the church are hosting a tea in Miss Bartlett's honor this afternoon. When I return from escorting her, would you accompany me to McSorley's? The ale, raw onions, and turkey all are first rate, I promise you. It's just we two. Tommy is busy with his studies."

"The villa's host is scorning the toque?"

"Alas, the host's culinary skills are so poor, even the lads on the roof won't touch his dinners."

"Then McSorley's it is."

"I shan't be long. If you like, you may play piano in the parlor. The music won't disturb Tommy. He's deaf in one ear."

The door closed, and John, deliberately ignoring the leaning floor and the scrabbling behind the faded wallpaper, wandered into the parlor.

80

For all its shabbiness, the flat was clean. Poverty, at least for the future Mr. and Mrs. Helsby, didn't equal substandard housekeeping, although the abode could have used a picture here and there and perhaps a potted plant or two to lighten its bleakness.

A small upright that shouted "scrap heap" pressed against one wall. John plunked a yellow key and winced at its reply. Taking a pass on torture, John gazed out the window and tried to envision what Savannah might be doing. Next year, John vowed, Helsby and his wife would spend their summer at the farm. He wondered if either of them could ride. Well, no matter. Between him and Savannah, it would simple to teach...

"Well, this is truly a first: Master John and a silent piano occupying the same room. I'd not have believed if my own eyes hadn't witnessed it."

John started from the reverie and turned from the window. "I didn't hear you come in."

"I'm quieter than mice. Ready?"

"Yes. Are we walking?"

"No, it's too far. I've called for a cab. And no, you shan't pay for it. It's my treat. I've been saving for it."

Lined up on the sidewalk outside the pub at 15 East 7th Street were empty barrels, all bearing the lettering *McSorley's.* The sign above the door extended from one end of the building to the other and read, *McSorley's Old Ale House: Established 1854.* Inside, sawdust covered the dark wood floors; tintype photographs and Harrigan and Hart playbills lined the walls. After inquiring if John would prefer the porter or the cream ale, Helsby ordered for them both and found a table.

"So don't be mum, Master John. What's her name?"

"Savannah Holloway."

Helsby leaned forward, eyes alight, the color rising in his cheeks. "The robber baron's widow?"

Inwardly, John smiled. He had forgotten Helsby's fascination with society news.

"The very same, Helsby."

"However did you meet her? Through your father?"

"You could say that."

Their meal arrived. Each man bowed his head for a silent prayer. After swallowing a generous forkful of turkey, Helsby asked, "And you're actually engaged?"

"Yes."

He shook his head and cut another slice. "A pity she had a conflict, but I suppose she must be quite occupied with finances. Mr. Holloway had amassed a substantial fortune."

"My interest is Savannah, not her money."

Astonished, Helsby set the fork down. "I never meant to imply otherwise. I only wished to say her affairs must keep her busy. But, as they say, marriage requires many sacrifices, and they often begin well before the 'I do's.'"

"So it seems, Helsby, so it seems."

That night, both Helsby and his brother bundled on the floor, in total agreement that the guest should have the bed. John was already regretting not staying at Sturtevant House. For one, he didn't feel comfortable allowing the groom-to-be to sleep on the floor in his own house on the eve of his wedding, but neither Helsby nor Tommy seemed to mind. Secondly, the scratching behind the walls unnerved him, and he feared that, if he did lie on the floor, tiny feet might patter across him while he slept, although the wobbly bed didn't feel safe, either. Finally, John, missing Savannah, folded a pillow over his head to block out Tommy's snoring, the shouting in the streets, and a dog that wouldn't shut up. He fell into a fitful sleep after the parlor clock chimed twice.

John awoke the next morning to the sound of Helsby humming the wedding march as he buttoned his ruffled shirt in front of the looking glass. Tommy had already vacated the room. John pushed the bedclothes away, and Helsby smiled.

"Ah, Master John, you're awake. Isn't it a glorious morning?"

"I'm happy for you, Helsby."

"There's bread and milk in the kitchen. Eat all you wish." Helsby reached for his cravat and slid it around his neck. "The real feasting comes this afternoon. The parents of my students are hosting a party for us in the church basement. A couple of them have already whisked Miss Bartlett away so I don't see her before the ceremony. They say it's bad luck."

"Superstitious?"

Helsby paused in mid-knot and looked up, considering. "Never thought about it." He resumed the tying. "In this case, I think it's more a matter of Miss Bartlett wishing to surprise me with her turned dress. Several ladies have worked very hard on it."

John stood and stretched. "You've lost me, Helsby. What's a 'turned dress?'"

Helsby reached for his suspenders. "A dress worn inside out."

John stopped stretching. "You're jesting!"

"I absolutely am not. Clothing fades from the outside. The inside fabric is clean and bright. Trim it with ribbons and lace, and voila! A new dress, and no one is wiser." He fastened the chain of his pocket watch and checked the time. "Master John, I must hurry. The parson wishes to speak to me before the wedding commences. You can't miss the church. It's straight down 11th."

"I'll be there Helsby."

"Ten sharp."

"I know."

John found the Methodist Episcopal Church with no trouble. The Gothic Revival structure discreetly sat amongst buildings that comprised 11th Street. The full church gave John a good excuse to witness the vows from the narthex, where he could slip out if missing Savannah grew unbearable.

Near the front, a young girl, about twelve, most likely a student from Helsby's school, plunked out a sampling of hymns on a cheap piano. The narthex door opened, and the girl abruptly switched to *The Wedding March*. Felicity appeared on Tommy's arm, looking sweet in organdy, the inside seams inconspicuously trimmed with the same tulle as her veil. Her sole ornaments were the gardenias she wore about her waist and tucked in her hair, a surprise gift from John, which he had ordered from Virginia before Abbott had sent him to New Haven. Felicity left their fragrance behind her as she minced down the aisle to join Helsby.

John stood too far away to hear most of the repetitions, but when it came time for Felicity to say, "I do," she did so with an exuberance that visibly moved more than Helsby, as several of the guests also dabbed at their eyes. When the parson announced, "You may kiss the bride," Helsby eagerly delivered the long-awaited kiss, which Mrs. Helsby returned with equal joy. John could only think of Savannah; with relief, he soon headed to the basement with the rest of the guests.

The food was simple, but plentiful: loaf pudding, pork and potato balls, fried corn patties, and plain cake. Cheap wine, as well as the many toasts for long life, good health, prosperity, happy years, flowed like water. Several of the fathers from the school could fiddle, so when the feast ended, they pushed the tables against the walls, and the dancing commenced. This was not the elegant dancing of Emily King's debutante ball, but boisterous, foot-stomping, hand-clapping dancing that produced red faces and plenty of huffing and puffing. As John watched, he wondered if he and Savannah might elope.

Later that evening, Helsby approached John with a limp roll of dollars.

"I've ordered a cab for you, Master John. I'd accompany you to the station, but I fear it would be most improper."

"Put your money away, Helsby, and use it on your family. I can well afford a cab."

"I feel badly about not accompanying you," Helsby said, glancing backward at Felicity as she danced a lively polka with Tommy.

"You belong with your wife tonight. No one would expect otherwise."

"Well," Helsby leaned close and giggled. "I *am* loath to leave her side, even for a minute."

"As it should be. Thank you for the privilege of sharing in your day. I'm humbled you'd want me here. I wish you a good life."

Helsby clasped John's hands in his. "We are better than brothers, Master John. I am your servant until death do us part."

"Likewise, Helsby."

The polka ended. Felicity eased her way through the crowds to Helsby just as John turned toward the door.

"You're leaving so soon?" Felicity looked up at Helsby with disappointed surprise and then at John. "I thought you'd stay another couple of days."

"No, I must go." John pulled her close and kissed her cheek. "Take care of this idiot tutor of mine. He depends on you more than you could know."

"I do, indeed," Helsby said, beaming at Felicity and pulling her tight. "I do, indeed."

"Congratulations, again," John said.

The ride to New Haven, long, dark, and weary, first by cab and second by train, was, nevertheless, a joyful one, for each mile conquered brought John closer to Savannah. Too agitated to sleep, John contemplated his star and replayed the events of the last day and the one before that, rolling the memories backward in his mind as the train sped toward John's future.

He jerked awake as the train pulled into the depot. The platform was deserted save for the few passengers that exited, but the cab was waiting for him, just as he had ordered. He dozed off several times as it bumped along to the farm, coming to foggy consciousness in time to see the outline of the barns against the midnight horizon. As soon as it stopped, John bounded out of the cab, shoved a fistful of bills into the driver's hand, and sprang up the rear steps, only to meet resistance.

The door was locked.

Disbelieving, John tried the knob again. Definitely locked, but logical. Savannah was alone, without any male protection, in this vast open space. He set the suitcase on the ground and wandered about the farmhouse, searching for an open window. He found it near the cellar. He crawled inside, felt his way in the dark for the staircase, and crept upstairs to Savannah. That's when John received a second surprise.

Her bedroom, also locked.

Softly, John knocked, not wishing to jar her.

Nothing.

John knocked a little louder, and, when that did not work, he rapped hard.

Nothing.

Irritated now, John banged on the door. Instantly, Savannah cracked it open, pulling her dressing gown closed with the other hand. She wasn't afraid. She was seething.

"Savannah, what is going...?"

Between clenched teeth, Savannah hissed, "How'd you get in?"

"The doors were locked, so I crawled in through the basement, and..."

"How dare you barge into my house and demand answers!" Savannah was still angry, still whispering. "Get out!"

His chest squeezed, and a whirlwind roared in his head, but he managed to choke out, "Why are you whispering?"

"I'm not whispering," Savannah hotly whispered back.

John knew the next question would shatter his fantasy but ask it he must. His voice raised a notch. "Is someone in your room?"

"What?"

With sickening realization, John cried out, "Someone's in there!"

"Get out of here!"

He tried to push past, but Savannah braced herself against the door. That movement shamed him into reality. His jealousy vanished. Now he understood this anger from. Savannah, soon-to-be his bride. He had doubted her, and she had responded to his doubt.

"Savannah, I'm sorry, I..."

Still glaring, her expression somewhat softened.

"You're right," Savannah whispered, but her voice was tense. "This...this is wrong." Distractedly, she shook her head. "Let me get dressed. I'll meet you in the drawing room."

"Savannah."

"Please," she whispered again, glancing over her shoulder. "I'll be right down."

"Sure."

Slowly, John descended the stairs with far less hope and enthusiasm than when ascending them. He lit the candelabra inside the drawing room and moved it to the piano, where he stood, absently plunking out the notes to the song Savannah had inspired. He gazed out the window, but saw only darkness. Dawn was hours away.

Savannah entered, dressed and perfectly groomed, holding a rosebud cup of tea in one hand and handing John a banknote with the other. Bewildered, John accepted it.

"I don't understand."

"Your pay," Savannah smiled, a cool unperturbed smile. "For your services this summer."

"My pay?"

A cough across the room made them both turn. A boy, about John's age, but with short and tousled hair and baggy breeches, stood in the doorway. His shirt gaped in the middle, where he had altogether missed a button.

"I...I'm sorry," the boy stammered. "I couldn't find the towels."

"First closet on the right past the bedroom," Savannah said with maddening tranquility.

The boy slunk away, and she crossed the room to shut the door. John's head spun, and his heart pounded faster than her footsteps. So this was how love ended? No heated argument or passionate declarations of fidelity unto death, just a fistful of cash and a calm dismissal? He watched her movements and remembered how he had...and how she had...and how the mere uttering of June, July, and August would now and forever crush his heart and how the remembrance of horses, blackberries, summer thunderstorms and summer weddings, would plague and sadden him all the days of his life.

"Savannah."

She turned, the arched eyebrows asking the question, the serene politeness of her face slashing his heart as if she'd dug a spur into it.

"Yes, John?"

He walked toward her, ripping the bank note into bits. Savannah sipped her tea and watched the shreds as they floated to the carpet.

John held up the last piece before her face. "Go to hell."

He let it drop, pushed past her, and exited the farmhouse in the direction of New Haven, breathing in the pure pre-dawn air. He now knew his purpose and felt ready to meet the hardships required to attain it. Never in his life did he so enjoy going home.

CHAPTER SIX: SHEDDING THE COCOON

If John had been any other young man, he would have rejoiced at the circumstances to which he had returned home. For when Abbott had promised to set John up in business, he hadn't meant to hire John. Abbott intended to give John the company and retire behind the scenes as a silent overseer.

Seemingly overnight, John's value had risen in Abbott's eyes. By spending the summer working for Savannah, John had proven that he could obey his father's wishes and that Abbott could shape him into the most worthy successor of F.A. Simons and Company. Reassured and encouraged, Abbot gave John free and total access to all business records and contacts and placed John by his right at board of trustee meetings - even when Lord Girard attended - and all interactions with the public.

Yet the more Abbott opened his accounts to his only son, the more John resented it. One, John's plans to lay siege against and then plunder his father's capital had withered without a whimper. He couldn't feel victorious over booty voluntarily laid before his feet, with blessings. Two, he had no release for his frustrations. He shunned the drawing room as he might a home with a quarantine notice posted on its door. He'd played every note on the scale for Savannah, and the sound of any of them drove hot pokers into his heart.

You're here to work?
To work...and to learn.

His post-Wesley education proved a costly one, and John took no comfort in mastering its lessons. Yes, sleeping in barns, frequenting Queens, and surviving the venomous bite of Black Widow had fashioned a great stamina for privation and vicissitude. Unfortunately, each step away from New Haven was also a step down the ladder he had constructed toward his musical legacy. Having lost sight of the top, John desperately clung to the rung his father had forged and cursed the day of his conception.

"God damn it!"

John spluttered into his coffee. "What?"

Abbott slapped the newspaper onto the table. "King's oldest daughter is engaged."

"Emily?" John dabbed the tablecloth with his napkin. "To whom?"

"A cousin of the Vanderbilts."

"What's the problem? You drool over the Vanderbilts."

Abbott glared at John. "You're missing the point. I wanted an alliance between Jacob King's family and ours."

"Yes, because America is so medieval."

"You don't find Miss King agreeable? The two of you were rather tight at her debutante ball."

John slowly swallowed the mouthful of strawberries. So much had happened since that ball.

"Surprised I knew that, eh? Are you going to deny it?"

"I'm happy for the Kings and the Vanderbilts."

In reality, John had only experienced two sources of happiness: music and Savannah, and both were gone. What a fool he'd been to entwine the two! Fortunately, a mind filled with columns of figures, renewable loans, and shareholder dividends left little time to imagine Savannah's nuzzling her newest stable boy; a day filled with meetings and a night reviewing statements meant John could avoid his mother's hothouse chambers indefinitely.

A knock halted his thoughts.

"Come in!"

Talbert bore the breakfast tray and a copy of the New York Gazette. With Abbott out of town again until tomorrow, John had no reason to take meals in the small dining room, as if Lucetta would join them. Better to remain in his rooms and have the necessities brought to him. Talbert read the day's itinerary as John sat by the open window, sipped his first cup of coffee, and scanned the morning's headlines.

"I recommend leaving within the hour," Talbert said, as he laid the schedule by the tray.

"I planned on it."

"Enjoy your breakfast, sir. Ring when you're ready to shave and dress."

A cooler breeze fluttered past the curtains today, a sure sign autumn was snuffing out the last breath of a summer he needed to die. John raised the lid and sampled the buckwheat cakes without tasting them.

The day was an everlasting succession of meetings and customer complaints. As he packed his briefcase, a hearty, "Halloo, John," caused a fleeting upward glance before resuming his task.

"Whatever you're selling, I'm not buying," John said.

"I'm not selling a thing." Mortimer Rutherford perched on the end of John's desk. "I'm opportunity, and I knock but once."

"Suit yourself, John, but remember this." She glanced over her shoulder. "I don't offer twice."

John snapped the case shut. Mortimer slid off the desk and traipsed behind him, through the halls and into the main lobby, his shoes squeaking like a nest of mice across the waxed floor

"What would you say," Mortimer said, breathless, as he caught John's sleeve, "if I told you a certain couple was making preparations for a lavish Valentine's Day party to celebrate their twenty-fifth anniversary?"

"I'd say, 'Happy anniversary.'"

The head cashier nodded to John as he passed. "Good night, Mr. Simons."

A door pushed open, and John stepped outside. Mortimer slid between him and the waiting carriage and thrust a finger in John's face. "And what if I told you they were willing to pay out the ass for quality entertainment?"

"Move or be removed."

"And what if I told you I happened to know the audition schedule. And that I've secretly arranged for you to arrive ahead of time and beat them all?"

Savannah leaned over the piano, wine glass in hand...God, she was beautiful...

John's throat tightened. He looked away.

Mortimer squealed and cried, "Aha! I knew it." He waved a piece of paper before John's face. "The address is at the bottom. Arrive half an hour before the first one, and, I guarantee, they won't hear another."

John pushed the paper away. "Good night."

He stepped into the waiting carriage, leaving Mortimer to gape and stare like a hooked trout. But as the vehicle took its place in the late afternoon traffic, the distinct tones of a waltz played by a Schwechten piano broke loose inside John's mind, and he closed his eyes against the anguish. Instinctively, John clenched his fists and squeezed his eyelids. When the storm receded, John moved aside the curtain and dully gazed at the honking geese and then at the ground as the carriage rumbled past Central Park, brilliant in gold, coral, and crimson. Acorns scattered like dusty chocolate hid the fading turf, a reminder to four-footed inhabitants to commence winter preparations. John watched the scene and burned with envy at the freedom of birds and squirrels. A crescendo and the chords ended.

"Paxton," John said as Paxton met him at the door and removed his coat and hat. "Send word to Mortimer Rutherford to meet me at the bank tomorrow morning."

"Right away, sir. What time will you dine, so I can alert the staff?"

"I'll let you know."

John headed straight for the drawing room.

The next morning, Mortimer was fairly tap dancing in the lobby. Without acknowledging the other man, John proceeded to his office, waited until Mortimer cleared the threshold, and then firmly shut the door.

"What is your interest in helping me?" John asked as he walked to his desk.

"Purely benevolent."

John flipped open his briefcase and began sorting its contents. "Again, what is your interest in helping me?"

"My, my so mistrustful."

"We're done." John started for the door.

Mortimer held up his hands. "Okay, okay, Twenty percent."

"Good-bye."

"Fifteen?"

John headed for the door. Mortimer did, too, flattening himself against it.

"I'll settle for ten, even five!"

John's hand reached for the knob, but Mortimer grabbed his wrist.

"Why let money divide friends? Seriously, John, this is a good deal for you." Mortimer waved his hands back and forth. "This...this bank and the lifestyle accompanying it. Maybe it's good enough for Farlow Abbott Simons, but it's refuse for the protégé of Maestro Seymour Cassidy. Look at yourself in the glass, John. You feel trapped. It plainly shows on your face."

"For the last time, Mortimer, what is your interest in helping me?"

Mortimer cleared his throat. "Gambling debt."

"And whose anniversary party?"

"My parents."

John shoved him to the ground and flung open the door.

"Come on, John! Reconsider!"

"Leave now, or you'll add jail time to your list of offenses."

"Fine," Mortimer struggled to his feet and dusted off his trousers. But he did set a folded sheet of paper on John's desk. "Just in case you change your mind. If you go, and I'm stressing the 'if,' please remember me with a small percentage of the earnings, a little gift, as it were."

John returned to the drawing room in the evenings, but he forced himself to be technical, objective, detached. One night, while just sitting, not thinking, not playing, the door opened, and a dim flame softened the darkness.

"Oh, excuse me sir," the chambermaid cried. "I didn't know anyone was here."

John wearily rose and shut the lid. "I was just leaving."

She curtsied, moved to the next lamp, and lit it. Plump like a bird, but with a round face and a starched white cap hiding most of her black hair, this girl had nothing of Nora's agility and grace, although her steady movements indicated punctuality and faithfulness. John hesitated. He didn't feel like staying, and neither did he feel like returning to his chambers. He could visit Lucetta, but her empty mind unsettled him more than his empty rooms.

"Are you new?" John asked.

She paused, panic in her black eyes. "Sir, did you speak to me?"

John took a step forward, and the girl took one back.

"Don't be afraid," John said. "You are not in trouble. In fact, you appear rather industrious, a commendable trait in a servant."

The girl relaxed, slightly.

"I am new," she whispered. "Just two weeks."

"Two weeks?" John feigned surprise. "And you've perfected your duties? What a clever girl!"

She blushed and moved to the next lamp. John moved with her.

"What is your name?" he asked.

With a trembling hand, she unscrewed the chimney.

"Bryga." She kept her eyes on the glass. "Bryga Bednarczyk."

"Well, Bryga. I shall inform my father of your attentiveness to the lamps."

Bryga blushed again, harder this time. "Thank you, sir."

"Ahem!"

Both John and Bryga started and turned toward the voice. Paxton stood in the doorway.

"Dinner is ready, sir. Will you join your father in the dining room, or shall I send a tray to your room again?"

"Tell my father I'll join him presently."

Discussing the evening news was preferable to the clamoring of searing memories.

"Very good, sir."

Thanksgiving brought the usual ostentatious guest list to enjoy an Abbott Simons spread: cream of celery soup, deviled oysters, roast duck and roast turkey, boiled turnips, mashed sweet potatoes, plum pudding, fresh breads and an assortment of cream pies besides the pumpkin. Yet John scarcely noticed the company or the food, so absorbed was he in his plans. The next morning, John realized he'd forgotten to see Lucetta and hoped, as he trotted down the stairs and away to work, one of the servants had remembered to feed her.

A week later, as John was standing inside the drawing room at the home of piano manufacturer Herbert Rutherford and fingering the keys of a Rutherford-designed upright, he heard a deep voice exclaim, "Oh, hell, no!"

A second voice, feminine, called from outside the door, "Mr. Rutherford, what are you moaning about now?"

John stopped playing, straightened, and took his first look at Mortimer's father. Herbert was a short boxy man with glistening dark hair and a twitchy handlebar mustache. The woman, handsome and willowy, with a crown of champagne braids encircling her head and diamonds hanging from her ears, around her neck, and bedecking most fingers, glided into the room.

"Gracious, have the auditions begun?"

"He's not auditioning," Herbert reached for the cord. "That's Abbott Simons' boy. The last thing I need is to piss off the president of the bank that holds my loans. I'm having Connors throw him out."

"Oh," the woman said with a surprised little gasp. "Why, husband dear, he's Seymour Cassidy's apprentice. I've so wanted to hear him play."

Herbert grunted as a uniformed servant appeared in the doorway. "Well, today's not the day. Connors, show this young man the door."

"Just a moment." The woman turned back to John. "Is it your desire to play for my party?"

"It is."

"And you prepared an audition piece?"

"No. I wrote a song especially for your anniversary."

"Oh, my!"

"Della, for God's sake," Herbert began.

"Mr. Rutherford," Della said, but her eyes were on John. "Since the young man is here, what harm is there in allowing him to present it? After all, he did compose it for us."

"Fine," Herbert said in a tone that showed it was not fine. He flung a hand into the air. "Connors, that will be all."

Connors bowed and left. Glancing at Della, then to Herbert and then at Della again, John seated himself at the piano...and froze. He couldn't do it; he had to do it; he launched into the song finally completed, weeks later, far away from Connecticut farms where Savannah would never hear it. Its melody infused the room and whisked John to
straw-colored hair piled under a wide-brimmed straw hat...
hazel eyes twinkled with amusement...
held out her gloved hand...
put her hands on his shoulders...
raised her eyebrows...
smiled, a half smile of surprise and intrigue...
grasped his face and eased it from side to side, as she bit her lower lip...
dazzling in white linen, trimmed in tiny buttons and ruffles at the high collar and wrists...
face framed by a few rebel tendrils from her regal pompadour...

92

caressing a glass of burgundy wine...
dreamy eyes...
face softened...
eyes brightened...
grinned with girlish delight...
leaned forward and motioned with her finger...
moved aside his hair and brought her lips to his ear...
hair tumbled down...
with a rapturous smile...
turned her face to the ceiling and closed her eyes...
opened her eyes and looked at...placed a hand on his...
brushing one of the thoroughbreds...
shrugged and held out an apple...
wrapped in charcoal blue and barely pink...
beige ruffles at the collar, shoulders, wrists, hem, and down the middle...
brushed away cascading hair...
accepted the cup with one hand while yawning into the back of another...
two hands around as she blissfully sipped....
tracing gold lines with a finger...
lost in reminiscing...
cupped her hands and drank...
stretched out in the grass, flung her arms above her head...
a full deep melodious laugh...
reached out and tweaked his cheek...
crawled away on hands and knees...
pressed the fruit between his lips...
briefly parted her lips...
quickly dismounted...
rapidly unbuttoned her shirt...
kicked off her boots...
stepped out of her pants...
twisting water from her hair...
face in his hands...
forcefully kissing...
held her fast...
entwined her fingers in his hair...
threw a strong leg over his waist, and scooted closer...
pointed out each item...
tilted her head and smiled teasingly...
mouth was full of mirth...
leaned over the piano, wine glass in hand...
mist in her eyes...
pulled her tight and tasted salt...

stirred, stretched, and smiled at him...
playful smile...
climbed to her knees and threw her arms around his neck...
tossed her head...
kissed her again, easing her back onto the bed...
curled against him...
a shadow crossed her face, and she said no
more..

Not until his fingers touched the final notes did John realize he was sitting in the Rutherfords' drawing room. He paused, hands in lap, and then raised his eyes, sheepish and exposed. Della was leaning over the piano and studying him, incredulity, wonder, and awe written on her face. Eternity passed between her cerulean eyes and his lighter ones, a stillness of peace and repose, a wordless reading of his soul.

Abruptly, Della rose, snapping their connecting thread as she looked at her husband.

"He plays," Della said.

Head high, she turned on her heel and stalked out of the room.

By next week, Christmas cards from business associates were pouring into the house. Abbott shook his head when he saw another stack sitting on his desk and pushed them aside.

"It's Louis Prang's contest, that's what it is," Abbott grumbled as he settled in the chair with his fourth cup of coffee. "There you have it, John, the common man, hoping to make an uncommon mark with a lousy piece of art and another mercenary transaction for a holyday."

John picked up one such L. Prang and Company card. A red-head angel, hands on her hips, with a Xmas banner on the top right and a "to and "from" on her lower left smirked back at him.

"You don't feel Jay Gould is sincere? Shocking!" John tossed the card on the desk. "Still, you don't mind yet another shipment of German mercury glass for your annual round of New Haven blue spruces, one for every wing of every floor, if I'm correct, courtesy of Uncle Ralph."

Still intent on the account books, Abbott muttered, "We do an extraordinary amount of entertaining."

"Explains your concern regarding insufficient alms for the poor."

"That reminds me," Abbott said, glancing up with sly eyes. "Your pay is reduced for this month. I figured you'd want to make a generous contribution to Hudson Poor Farm, current home of the Gibbs family."

John held the gaze, but inside, he boiled with fury. Without another word, he left the room.

By the evening of December 23, the house was filled with guests anticipating festivities extending through New Year's Day, most of them

94

centered around food, from the creamed fish leading the Christmas Eve dinner at dusk to the roast goose stuffed with apples and potatoes on Christmas evening. As Christmas Eve night deepened and the post-dinner conversations grew louder over thick slices of Irish cake and lively games of whist, John retreated to his chambers, avoiding those of his mother's where she relentlessly sang *Silent Night*, to think and plan.

He was back downstairs by a quarter past eleven. With his star outshining the others in brilliance and brightness, John accompanied Abbott on foot to the candlelit midnight Mass at Old St. Patrick's Cathedral. Abbott stubbornly refused to set foot inside the new seat of the Archdiocese of New York, which John could not comprehend, as his father was not generally sentimental. But either the solemnity of the newborn Savior or the claret punch struck Abbott, for his strong tenor cut through the silent, glittering night on the walk back:

Adeste, fideles, laeti triumphantes:
Venite, venite in Bethlehem:
Venite adoremus.
Venite adoremus.
Venite adoremus Dominum.

At home, feast number two awaited them: French omelets, hot buttered toast, buckwheat cakes, creamed potatoes and creamed sweetbreads, oyster pie, assorted jellies, and coffee. But the post-Mass discussions were subdued and halting. Gradually, the weary clan dispersed to their rooms, and John went with them, *Gloria, in excelsis Deo* lingering in his mind. By late morning, they had relished a hearty brunch of French onion soup, mutton chops, and fried apples; an afternoon Christmas tea staved off hunger pains for several more hours. John retired sooner than usual. Abbott had scheduled an early morning meeting with the board of trustees.

On Saturday, the last day of the year, Abbott closed the bank at noon and donned his best host etiquette for yet another multi-coursed feast in the large dining room and musical entertainment in the drawing room. John sat in the corner and greeted eighteen eighty-two with a bottle of champagne and a heart of steel. He'd erred greatly in softening toward Savannah. He would never make that mistake toward any woman again.

Never.

The crowd sang Auld Layne Syne; a cloud drifted over his star.

Immediately after breakfast on the Saturday before the Rutherford's party, John called a cab and drove into Queens, where he made reservations, signed contracts, and promised payments within the week. Back in upper Manhattan, John stopped at the print shop before returning home. On Sunday, he attended High Mass at Old St. Patrick's Cathedral with Abbott. Its Federal-style architecture and plaster ceiling and walls still resembled home: hard, beautiful, and cold. Beside him, Abbott stood as erect and immobile as the marble statues, but not nearly so tall. To the accompaniment of the Erben organ, Abbott sang those majestic Latin hymns in a strong and powerful tenor voice. On the way home, Abbott tossed a coin at a ragged boy with a runny nose in exchange for the latest edition of the New York Gazette and sneered at the new and official cathedral.

At noon the next day, Abbott sent John home, a supportive move that momentarily disarmed John, before he dismissed it as too little, too late. Still, John used this time to refine his selections. Tonight he would play his first and sole concert on this end of the state. It should be a memorable one, starting with his dress.

While the other men would wear black trousers and tailcoats, black, gray, or silver waistcoats; and white wing-collar shirts, ties, and gloves. John would wear all white, a silent means of communicating to the guests the unusualness of the performance. As John had requested, Della had provided a copy of the invitation and the guest list. Many were his father's colleagues. Good.

John arrived promptly at seven, about half an hour before the other guests arrived, so he could ensure drawing room preparations were suitable for the post-dinner concert. He stayed near the mantle in the formal parlor, poised for Della's announcement. In a shimmery gown of silver and mauve, Della stood near the parlor entry, greeting each couple, handing them a slip of paper, and ushering them inside.

A tubby man adjusted his monocle, unfolded his paper, and read aloud, "What is your wife's favorite flower?"

"That's easy," Herbert said, "The iris." He peered over the monocle man's shoulder. "No Lord Girard?"

The monocle dropped. "No, he left for the country this morning."

"Mr. Brumfeldt, I can't say I blame him," Genevieve Harrington cooed from the sofa, left hand gracefully draped over the chair's padded arm, pale ringlets plastered in perfect form on her forehead. "Arcadia is perfectly divine."

Brumfeldt replaced the monocle. "It's bitter cold, and the grounds are buried under snow."

"I'm well aware, Mr. Brumfeldt, but I daresay the view from the east morning room on the first floor is rather magical, what with the snow-dipped shrubbery, frosted branches, and dawn's pink sun casting sparkles over the terrain."

Brumfeldt stared at Genevieve in stunned disbelief. No one spoke. Herbert broke the silence by saying, "Mr. Smythe, I believe it's your turn."

The short and shrunken Bartholomew Smythe grasped his sheet with shaking hands, and read in a raspy voice, "Describe Mrs. Rutherford's wedding gown."

A murmur spread through the room, and all feminine eyes turned on Herbert, who accepted another cocktail from the tray as his butler made the rounds, and took a sip.

"I never noticed the gown," Herbert said smoothly. "Only her radiance."

Mortimer, looking dapper in his new sideburns and French coat, glanced away from his earnest conversation with his fiancé and snickered. Edwina Smythe, as slight as her husband, a severe gray bun atop her small head, turned away from the Monet she was studying to raise her glass in approval. "Very eloquent, sir."

Herbert beamed over his glass.

"Well, then, Rutherford," Marshall Harrington stroked his black horseshoe mustache. "Does your lovely bride prefer the country or the seashore?"

"I should think t'wouldn't matter," Herbert took another sip. "As long as I am there."

"Mr. Rutherford, you are indeed incorrigible," but Genevieve's smile belied her disapproving words.

Della returned in a swish of satin. "Mr. Rutherford, have you introduced our esteemed guest?"

Herbert held out his glass. "Dearest, you may have the honor."

Della rustled to the mantle and linked her arm in John's.

"Ladies and gentlemen," Della said with a bright smile. "For those of you unacquainted with Mr. Abbott Simons' son, Maestro Seymour Cassidy's protégé, and recent graduate of Wesley Conservatory of Music, I'd like you to meet the much-esteemed Mr. John Simons. He will join us for dinner and entertain us later tonight."

The butler appeared in the doorway. "Dinner is served."

Della's arm remained looped in John's. "Please escort me to the dining room."

The servants had arranged the room with a dozen tables covered in white damask and place settings for eight. In the center of each stood tiered bowls of fresh fruit and white tapers, which the servants were lighting. A swan napkin perched on top of each gold-rimmed plate and guarded the army of silverware. After helping Della to her seat and taking his place on her right, John glanced at the menu:

Consommé
Assorted Pickles
Foie Gras
Poached fish with lobster Sauce
Rum Sorbet
Roast pheasant with Potatoes in Jackets
Celeriac and Tart Apple Puree
Green Salad
Chantilly Cheese and Brandied Fruit

"Frightful affair, isn't?" Mortimer said from across the table, to no one in particular. "Another evening of dyspepsia, thank you Pierre."

Herbert glared at Mortimer, who smiled benignly at his father, as he tucked his napkin into his shirt, and said, "All in the name of true love, of course." He covered his fiancé's hand. "Wouldn't you agree, Trixie, er, Miss Beatrice?"

Miss Beatrice bowed her red curls and blushed.

Most of the dinner conversation revolved around the financial trade, for Bartholomew Smythe was also a banker, and Marshall owned the international investment firm of M. Harrington & Sons. John, who'd eaten his fill of figures and funds, still would not allow his mind to drift, for, like a rebellious homing pigeon, his thoughts always returned to New Haven. Instead, John concentrated on each course placed before him and feigned attention, until Marshall accepted a slice of pheasant with a, "Damn shame about Holloway."

"Caught the grippe, didn't he?" Herbert asked. "Pity to have amassed billions and then depart from this world without their full enjoyment."

"If you ask me," Mortimer said, although no one had. "I think the old man was foolish retiring to the country, away from civilization and New York medicine, isn't that right, Mr. Smythe?"

"I'm not against the country," Bartholomew croaked, pausing to cough into his napkin. "It offers pleasantries unique to that domain."

"T'would be mighty hard to treat your croup out there."

Edwina leaned forward, eyes sparking. "*We* never travel without our private physician. *We* learned from Mr. Holloway's lapse in good judgment."

"I wouldn't slam his judgment," Marshall grinned, his eyes darting over the other men. "After all, he did marry quite the young looker."

A stream of male laughter followed. Della halted their merriment with, "Didn't she have ties to the Carnegies?"

"I never said I attended the circus. I said I met him at the circus."

98

Curiosity replacing timidity, John lay down to face her and propped his head with one hand. "Seems to me attending would be a requirement."

A sly look appeared in Savannah's eyes. "Not when one works for Mr. Barnum."

John blinked. "You worked for his circus?"

"I was a bareback lady."

"A bareback lady."

"Yes, on an elephant." Savannah laughed, a full deep melodious laugh.

"You made that up!"

"Speaking of the Carnegies," Marshall said, "I hear Andrew Carnegie has an interest in the Frick Coke Company."

"Salad?" the footman asked John.

Throat tight, John managed a strangled, "Sure."

"You're right." Savannah glanced away. "I shouldn't be alone. "Far too many memories."

John gently grasped her cheeks and made her face him. He kissed her again. "Then let's make new ones."

"So what was it like?" Marshall asked.

Every head turned in John's direction. He slid the plate of Chantilly cream and brandied fruit closer to him and picked up a spoon. "Like?"

"Working so closely under Maestro Cassidy's direction," Genevieve said. "I'd heard him play in Europe. He had phenomenal talent. One can only imagine being under his tutelage."

WHACK!

John drew back his right hand and rubbed it with his left. "I doubt you'd smack Mozart."

"Mozart was a genius. You are not."

"Unforgettable," John said.

Brumfeldt's other eye grew large. "Indeed!"

Genevieve swallowed the last bite and pushed aside her plate. "I'm much curious if Maestro's genius resides in you."

Della caught John's eye and smiled at Genevieve. "I think Mr. Simons will impress you."

The footmen began distributing water bowls. Herbert dipped his fingers and rose.

"Time to let the ladies talk before the show begins. Wait until you taste the white port I ordered for tonight. Why it's..."

Della leaned close to John and murmured, "Nervous?"

"No."

By the time John took his place at the piano, snuff boxes were being freely distributed and the port was disappearing at a rapid rate. Even the wedding cake, just tall enough for Herbert to stretch over it and reprise the kiss he had first given Della twenty-five years ago, had receded to bottom layers. Yet, as John reached the second half of the Savannah's song, all activity ceased in favor of the piano's heart-wrenching refrains. As the concert progressed, Mortimer, glass in hand, watched John with a thoughtful demeanor. Miss Beatrice had nodded to sleep in one of the love seats.

At the party's conclusion, John exchanged calling cards with the guests, accepted his generous pay from Herbert, counted out twenty-five percent into Mortimer's astonished hand, and then accepted a congratulatory glass of port. He'd done it.

The next morning, John again rode to Queens and settled his debts. He was back before noon, a brand-new cloak hanging over his arm.

"Wait here," John told the driver. "I'm leaving shortly."

John walked into the house just as Bryga crossed the hall to the main dining room. John motioned her to follow as he headed for the stairs. Dumbfounded, she just stood.

"Come with me," John called back, as he sped to the second floor. "I must speak to my father."

Outside Abbott's office, John handed Bryga the cloak. "Hold this. I'll return presently."

Head to forehead, face furrowed in deep thought, Abbott never looked up until John lifted a paperweight off the desk and let it drop. Abbott leaped to his feet, shoved the account books aside, and frantically examined the desk for nicks and scratches.

"What is the meaning of this?" Abbott demanded.

"I'm leaving."

"You bet your sweet ass you're leaving. Why aren't you at the bank? Did you forget Lord Girard's meeting?"

"That's why I chose today."

Wariness crept into his father's eyes. "Today?"

John heard the fear in his father's voice, too.

"I'm moving, to lower Manhattan. Instead of pandering to your clients, I'll be enticing customers through the doors of Hewes Music Hall."

Abbott's jaw dropped. Gaping, he inched toward John and searched his face.

"You've lost your mind," Abbott whispered.

"Actually, no. I've found it."

"You're really leaving?"

"Yes, sir. But you may visit."

Abbott's face contorted purple and red. He lunged at John, who nimbly stepped aside. Abbott banged the desk as he pointed his other finger and shouted, "I'll see you in hell first!"

"Looking forward to it, sir."

"Don't you dare take a single object from my house! Do you hear me, John? Nothing!"

"As you wish."

With a move reminiscent of St. Francis of Assisi, John stripped his garments, kicked them to his father's feet, and strode out of the room to a shocked Bryga, who quickly wrapped John in his cloak. No canticle of that great saint compared with the joyful song breaking forth in John's spirit as the carriage pulled out into the street, carrying a triumphant passenger, ready to embrace a leprous world.

CHAPTER SEVEN: MUSIC HALLS AND GARBAGE CANS

"Come in!"

The heavy door opened, and the ruddy face of Alfred Jackson poked into the room. Virgil Gundersmith, in checks and white cowboy hat, stopped fiddling, but Ebenezer "Benny" Brown, sequins sparking in the lamplight, coolly kept each ball orbiting above his head.

"Ten minutes, Johnny," Jackson said in unmistakable Cockney. "Ready?"

"Yes."

The fatigue fled. John rose from the old Windsor chair and adjusted his tails in the chipped and cloudy glass, while Jackson, looking more like an overinflated air ship than a man approaching middle-age, removed the flask from inside his pocket and took a large gulp. John couldn't help smiling. The reflection showed Dirk Meadows, one of the pantomime dames, peering at the cards of Polly Plese, a can-can girl, as the two played poker and smoked cigars with Obadiah Quill and Sally Lafayette, another can-can dancer.

"Break a leg, Johnny." Dirk's bulbous nose, five o'clock shadow, and Jack Spratt appearance contrasted with his upright pony tail and green satin gown.

"Thank you."

Obadiah, Dirk's "wife could eat no lean" counterpart, hairy arms bursting his light azure ruffled dress, merely said, "Raise."

As John and Jackson trotted toward the stage, Jackson said, "Mr. Hewes wants an extra performance tonight."

"Who's the no-show this time?"

"Cuddy Lane."

"Again?"

Jackson didn't reply, but John already knew the answer. Cuddy Lane, a ventriloquist, reappeared only when his beer money ran out.

They had reached the left wing. John peered into the auditorium. The balconies were nearly empty, the boxes completely so; the main floor was half full, with most of the patrons being men (with a fair amount being Chinese), sprawling with half-mast eyes. At least tonight all the tables were standing on four legs. At the upright piano in the center of the stage sat Archibald Stone, slick hair parted down the middle, full mustache wet with the rye whiskey of his cocktail, as he paused for another sip before launching into his final song of the evening:

By the light of a candle I happened to spy
A pretty young couple together did lie

The calliope tune rang through the theater. Jackson took another swig and wiped his mouth on his grimy coat sleeve, leaving a line of soot across his upper lip. John stood still, hands clasped behind his back.

Applause erupted. Archibald knocked back his drink, moved to center stage, bowed low and bowed again. Jackson dropped the curtain. The applause continued as Archibald sauntered into the wings.

"Top that, Johnny," Archibald smirked, pushing past him to the dressing room.

Jackson blew a raspberry. John smiled down at him, and Jackson grinned back. John didn't know why Jackson favored him, but considering he was the owner's cousin, John didn't discourage it. As Mr. Hewes once said, Jackson was loyal, and that blotted out his faults. The clapping died to nothing, and Jackson stuffed the flask in his pocket and raised the curtain. As John approached the piano, a hush spread through the crowd. John seated himself, paused and then launched into the solo portion of his new piano concerto.

Twenty minutes later, John exited to a round of half-hearted applause. Jackson capped the flask and dropped the curtain. Dirk and Obadiah stood in the wings, ready to perform.

"Better luck next time, Johnny," Dirk said.

John strode to the back of the theater. A panting Jackson trotted up to him.

"Blackguards, for not appreciatin' good music," Jackson gasped.

"It's been three months."

"Tykes time to train a man's ear." Jackson flung open the dressing room door. "Ten minutes, Benny. You ready?"

The juggler straightened his leotards and reached for his bag. His trunk of remaining implements was already near the stage.

"Urry," Jackson replaced the cap and nodded to John. "Up again in an hour."

Jackson shut the door behind him.

"Tough break, Johnny," Flossie McGee said, smoking a cigarette from her perch on the desk, knees drawn up to her chin.

Despite the regency wig, breeches, tall boots, and brass-buckled coat, Flossie exuded a sexual charm even Polly and Sally couldn't muster with swaggers, fishnets, and high leg kicks.

John sank into the settee. "What will it take?"

"Jackson is right." Flossie blew out a stream of smoke. "Takes time. These ain't the swells-lovin'-on-chamber-music at your Daddy's parties."

"They're also not devoid of culture, or they'd toss their coins at organ grinders."

Flossie grimaced and shifted position. "You're good, Johnny, real good. They'll come 'round."

"Dey git all da culture dey need," Bert Dobbins peeped over yesterday's New York Gazette with a wink, "once Flossie comes a-prancin' on stage. George the IV's got nuttin on Flossie's raunchiness."

Standing tall at just under five feet, Bert was the only other performer donned in tails, which elicited more laughs from the audience than his jokes did. However, Bert made a valid point. A first-rate male impersonator, Flossie drew almost as many patrons to Hewes Music Hall as Archibald Stone did, no matter what role she caricatured.

"I'm a better damn man than you'll ever be, Bertie," Flossie retorted, but she grinned as she said it.

"Should 'ope so." Bert returned to his newspaper. "I'm hunnerd percent Uranian."

The ruddy face of Jackson poked around. "Ten minutes, Flossie. You ready?"

Flossie snuffed out the cigarette and looked at John. "Think about what I said."

John leaned back; his head swam; and he *loped on his uncle's horse until the white farmhouse, trimmed in dark gray came into view, looking fresh and inviting in the early morning light. He rode straight back to the barns and meandered through the largest building, admiring the sleek thoroughbreds.*

"Well, well, what a surprise."

John's heart stopped. He spun around. Savannah's straw-colored hair was piled under a wide-brimmed straw hat. She unbuttoned her shirt and stepped out of her pants. God, she was beautiful. "I've always loved you, John."

He took Savannah's face in his hands and kissed her, never slowing, never stopping...

"Off to the loo," Obadiah called in the distance, "afore Flossie gits back."

A door closed; another banged open.

"Ten minutes, Johnny!"

Dazed, John opened his eyes, sleep *pulling him into straw...*

"Johnny!"

Jackson was bending over him, face frantic beneath his greasy cap, his breath smelling like the inside of a boot. "Aintcha ready?"

John smoothed his tails and plodded after Jackson, shaking weariness with every tripping step. After playing to a near-empty and far drowsier house, John dragged himself back to the empty dressing room, picked up his top hat and coat, and trudged up the fire escape stairs as they led to straight to his window, preferable to stepping over the derelicts in the hall. The scent of garbage and sewage wafted around him, but at least the air on this May night was light and cool, and he had the company of his star all the way. He forced up the window, crawled onto his bed, and rolled onto the floor. He lit a candle, and then he lit the stove. After reheating last night's gruel, John sat on the edge of the bed sucking the spoon, too tired to think. He woke when the bowl shattered on the boards. John kicked off his shoes, vaguely remembering to snuff out the candle before dropping onto the pillow.

A howling baby roused him. John buried his face into his pillow, futile against the loud bang from somewhere and the shrieks of slum children at play. Cramped from sleeping in one position all night, John slipped off the bed with a groan and staggered to the stove, thankful for running water, a luxury in lower Manhattan, one of the perks of living above the music hall. As the pot boiled, he added coffee, sliced half a loaf, grabbed a wedge of cheese from the icebox, and sat down to review his day: Two lessons, a parlor party, and then back to the music hall by nine o'clock. He'd discard all the side jobs once Dana Hewes increased his wages, but, first, John must improve his following. He had wowed them in upper Manhattan, although doors that once opened to John Simons, son of Abbott Simons, slammed once news of his estrangement spread through the city. Why couldn't he make it here?

John stuffed the last of the bread in his mouth and grabbed a towel. He had just slid into his shirt when the rapping began. John opened the door, and Tillie Davis stumbled in, carrying two large kettles. A rag wound around her left arm.

"Sorry I'm late," Tillie said. "Burned myself at breakfast and had to tie it up with ashes and lard."

Tillie began filling the kettles with water and setting them on the stove to boil.

"No matter," John said, buttoning his cuffs. "You'll have the place to yourself all day. I won't return until late."

"Don't you fret. I'll have everything cleaned and pressed long before you return." Beaming through broken and missing teeth, Tillie proudly added, "Teddy has already mastered yesterday's lessons, but don't tell him I squealed. It's his surprise."

Cringing in memory at the last lesson, John slid his tie around his neck and knotted it in a few swift moves.

"There's a bit of milk in the icebox, and you may have the last of the loaf." He picked up his overcoat coat and hat. "Don't forget to shut the window this time when you leave."

"Yessir." Tillie glanced across the room at the shattered bowl and the gruel smeared on the floor. "Fell asleep agin while eatin' dinner?"

Without answering, John closed the door behind him and tried not to brood. Despite careful monitoring of the money from the

Rutherfords' anniversary party, the stores were dwindling faster than John liked, the reason for the side jobs. While John would never hug a leper, he didn't mind pandering to them at reduced prices and pocketing their money.

He stepped outside and surveyed the morning scene. Men loitered in doorways and on stairwells; women with sagging and wrinkled skin leaned on windowsills and watched the foot traffic on the dusty streets: children hurried to school with book straps slung over their shoulders, husbands dashed to work, and housewives clutched shawls around their shoulders and peered into store windows. He didn't look at the sausage shop. The Helsbys had moved to the Central Park area right after Easter. They had found live-in positions, Andrew as a tutor and Felicity as a nanny.

The first lesson was inside another tenement apartment, not far from Hewes Music Hall. The children, a girl and two boys, along with their parents, were busy rolling cigarettes. This was no small operation; as a group, they turned out thousands each week, which the oldest boy sold on the streets as fast as the rest of the crew made them. It was this boy, Jake Haunch, about thirteen, who was John's pupil. When John entered the room, Jake dropped his work like a hot potato and hurried to the ancient piano, the family's most treasured possession.

"I kin play 'Mazin' Grace' right nice now." Jake positioned his fingers above the keys, not minding his dirty hands and the tobacco under his nails.

"Let's hear it," John said, eyes darting for a clean spot to set his coat and hat and deciding to keep them on his lap. The rest of the family continued to produce cigarette after cigarette with amazing speed.

Jake hadn't exaggerated, but, then again, Jake was John's best student. If Jake had a tuned piano and decent practice time, he might have developed his natural talent to a high degree. As the situation existed, the tune Jake played did, in fact, resemble *Amazing Grace*, so John pronounced that lesson mastered and turned to the next song in the tattered hymnal.

"This is Ma's favorite song," Jake remarked, as John began *Praise God From Whom All Blessings Flow.* "She's bin awaitin' fur me to learn it."

"Yes, indeedy." Mrs. Haunch kept rolling as she spoke. "We always thank the gid Lord for our blessins, especially for the muzak learnin' our Jakey is gittin, all due to your good heart, Mr. Simons."

"There," John said. "Now you try it, Jake."

An hour later, John was tucking the pouch into his coat pocket, bidding the family farewell and heading to his next lesson. This one was an hour away on foot to a dame school, where he spent the rest of the

106

afternoon teaching its five students, all girls, ranging in age from six to seventeen. After a fast supper consisting of pea soup and salt-raised bread, John took a Hansom cab to Ethan Damien's home, a local doctor entertaining his colleagues with an evening of chamber music in his parlor. An endless succession of requests caused the party to run late, and John arrived at the music hall fifteen minutes before show time. A frantic Jackson greeted him at the side door and traipsed behind John all the way to the green room

"Where ya been? Mr. Hewes was getting anxious-like. Wants you to play a second show. The fiddler didn't show."

"Virgil? I'm surprised. He never misses."

"Me, too, but he ain't here." Jackson knocked on the door and flung it open before anyone answered. "Five minutes, Johnny. Do what you gots to do."

Dirk and Obadiah were playing poker and smoking cigars with Polly and Sally. Benny was juggling, sequins from his costume flashing in the lamplight. Flossie sat hunched on the desk, picking at a bowl of gruel. John strode straight to the looking glass and started straightening his tails.

"Break a leg, Johnny," Dirk's bulbous nose and five o'clock shadow clashed with his floral kimono.

In the glass, John saw Dirk tap his cigar on the edge of the ashtray and peep at Polly's cards.

"Thank you," John said, brushing away lower Manhattan dust he had acquired from the coach seat.

Obadiah, puffed sleeves of his tight evening dress squeezing his upper arms, merely said, "Raise."

As John and Jackson sped to the stage, Virgil, coat tails flapping and clutching his fiddle, came running up.

"I can do my own spot tonight," Virgil panted. "I didn't have cab fare, and I had to pawn..."

"Sorry, you know Mr. Hewes' rules. Johnny here has already agreed..."

"He can play," John said.

Jackson stopped short, eyes wide, mouth open. "What?"

"Like I said, he never misses. Let him play."

Jackson looked confused. "But I already promised it to you."

Virgil set down the fiddle and grabbed John's hand with both of his and shook them hard. "Johnny, that's damn decent! Just for that, I'm gonna dedicate the first song to you."

The applause had begun. Archibald took one bow after another until Jackson recapped the flask and dropped the curtain. The applause continued as Archibald exited the stage.

"Top that, Johnny," Archibald smirked, pushing past him to the dressing room.

Jackson blew a raspberry and looked up at John, but John ignored the stage hand and studied the crowed. He would play to a full house tonight and almost regretted giving Virgil his spot back. When the clapping diminished, Jackson stuffed the flask in his pocket and raised the curtain. As John approached the piano, a hush spread through the crowd. John seated himself, paused, and launched into the solo piano excerpt of his new concerto.

Twenty minutes later, John exited to a round of half-hearted applause and a few boos. Jackson capped the flask and dropped the curtain. Dirk and Obadiah stood in the wings, ready to perform.

"Better luck next time, Johnny," Dirk said.

John strode to the green room. A panting Jackson trotted up to him.

"Blackguards, for not appreciatin' good music," Jackson gasped.

"Shut up."

"Huh?"

Jackson started to knock on the door, but John pushed it open and headed straight for his coat and hat. Near the back, Virgil was fiddling away as if the devil had demanded it.

"Ten minutes, Benny," Jackson pointed at him. "You ready?"

The juggler straightened his leotards, reached for his bag, and shut the door behind him

"Tough break, Johnny," Flossie McGee blew a steam of smoke from her perch on the desk.

John removed the Haunch's pouch of cigarettes from his coat pocket and tossed them to Flossie, who deftly caught them with her free hand.

"Whatever," John turned to leave.

"Come on, Johnny, stay and talk to your girl."

"Good night, Flossie."

John trudged up the fire escape stairs. The stink of garbage and sewage followed him; a cloud hid his star. He forced up the window, crawled onto his bed and off it again. He lit a candle, then the stove, and heated a batch of fresh gruel. John sat on the edge of the bed, picking at the slop, too tired to think, but at least he set an empty bowl on the floor tonight, instead of dropping a half-full one. John kicked off his shoes, snuffed out the candle, and fell asleep before his head touched the pillow.

Screaming from the apartment next door awakened John before he felt the sunlight from behind closed eyelids. Cramped from sleeping in one position all night, John rolled out of bed with a groan and staggered to the stove to start the coffee and a saucepan of porridge. When the toast was done, John sat down to his modest breakfast to review his day: Three lessons, but the last one was also an invitation to dinner. He'd have to monitor the time; his show was at nine o'clock.

John downed the last of the coffee and grabbed a towel. He had just finished dressing when Lila Davis, hair tied up in a kerchief, trotted in with a large overflowing sack. She set it on the table and began removing a loaf of bread, a string of sausages, and some potatoes.

"Just a little extra from our larder to yours," Lila said, "for all you've done for our Mary."

John turned his back as he reached for the tin coffee pot. "How many times have I told you to knock first?"

Lila didn't answer. John turned around. Lila was dragging a bucket and mop with her.

"I'd you offer lunch, but..."

"Sweetie, dontcha worry 'bout me. There'll be a nice surprise in the icebox when you return."

Once outside, John hailed a Hansom cab and settled into the seats, determined to ration both his energy and his sanity. He retained a certain sentimentality for ten-year-old Lonnie Russell, his first victim of the day, for the boy's father Leopold Russell, who had advertised in the New York Gazette for a piano tutor for his son, had banked at F.A. Simons & Company until his reversal in fortune last year. It gladdened John's spirit to teach the offspring of a former business associate of Abbott's, even if he was renting out rooms in his Fifth Avenue mansion to maintain his opulent lifestyle.

Lonnie, overfed both in body and ego, fancied himself John's equal and never practiced a lesson. Instead of the omission annoying John, the young Simons preferred it, for it meant minimal teaching effort with maximum pay.

"I'm a regular Brahms I am," Lonnie bragged as he ended the torture for the morning.

John said nothing, and Lonnie didn't notice.

Lesson number two was at the Burnerettas, a modest home where the mother supplemented her bookkeeper husband's income with sewing, not by hand, but through using an actual treadle sewing machine. His pupil was fifteen-year-old Elizabeth Burneretta, who worked as an elderly woman's companion and allocated some of her salary to pay for lessons. The employer had allowed Elizabeth to swap a weekday for an extra-long Saturday, especially since Elizabeth's playing soothed the old woman's fractious nerves. Consequently, Elizabeth was a proficient and conscientious student. Still, John loathed coming to this house, despite the fact Mrs. Rose Burneretta supplied a hearty soup and bread lunch before the piano tutorial began.

Ever intent on her work in an alcove off the parlor, Mrs. Burneretta somehow never heard the loud squabbling filling every hour of every piano lesson. Amazingly, Elizabeth could tune out her siblings, too, and continued to serenely play, never missing a note.

"Mine!" screeched Elizabeth's little sister Celia as she tugged on the rag doll, which an even littler sister had firmly grasped to her chest.

"Mine!" Mercy's teeth sank into Elizabeth's hand.

Elizabeth screamed, slapped Mercy, and yanked. Mercy toppled down and smacked her head on the piano leg.

"Mommy!" Still clutching the doll, Mercy ran for her mother.

The Watsons were too perfect to be true, the sort of family modeled in stories to teach children etiquette and morals. Three of the them - Garrett, nine; Benjamin, eight; and Eugenia, seven - received lessons from John, during which Baby Bonnie sat as still as a marble statue on Mrs. Flora Watson's lap and cooed with delight. The home, a parsonage, neither rich nor fashionable, was nevertheless warm and inviting, with its brushed carpet, polished furniture, and a tea table always set for the next guest. Garrett and Benjamin's wool suits (gray for Garrett and brown for Benjamin) were worn, but clean, and Eugenia, Baby Bonnie and Mrs. Watson's ribbons, (cobalt blue for Eugenia and Mrs. Watson, orchid for Baby Bonnie), both in hair and on dresses, were always fresh and crisp. Furthermore, the children displayed uncommonly fine manners and a spirit of sibling affection and cooperation.

"Lovely tune, brother dear," Eugenia clasped her hands in reverie, as Benjamin slid off the piano bench.

"Thank you, sister dear," Benjamin returned with a soft peck on her cheek, as Garrett crossed the room and assumed his seat, his back straight and fingers in proper position.

"I'm sure I shan't perform as well you two." Garrett gave a little bow. "But I shall try my best."

Mrs. Watson nodded her chair across the room and smoothed make-believe wrinkles from her gold and blue wrapper. "That's all God asks of us, my son."

Bonnie smiled and patted Mrs. Watson's cheek.

At the conclusion of *Our God in Help of Ages Past*, for the children were allowed to learn only hymns, the study door opened, and their father Pastor Milton Watson entered the room with a pleased smile on his face.

"What inspiration for Sunday's sermon, angelic music in the next room," Milton bent to kiss the top of his wife's head.

Still seated at the piano, Garrett blushed and bowed *his* head. Benjamin happily squirmed. Eugenia blushed. Mrs. Watson set Baby Bonnie on the floor, and the baby sat there, gazing around the room.

110

"From the pleasant aroma coming from the kitchen, Mrs. Catterling has prepared another fine dinner," Milton said. "John, you will stay and dine with us?"

"Of course," John said, starving for real food and wondering if he could endure any more syrup.

Mrs. Watson rose. "I shall inform Mrs. Catterling to set an extra place for our guest."

The evening meal was a long surreal affair. Although the food was modest servings of stewed chicken under biscuits and boiled cabbage, the Watson's served it with genuine love and partook of it with sincere appreciation to God for providing it and Mrs. Catterling for cooking it.

After a dessert of cream pudding, the Watsons pressed upon John to play and play again, so that when he rushed into the green room to check his tails, John bumped into an exasperated Jackson.

"I know," John said. "Five minutes."

Dirk and Obadiah were playing poker and smoking cigars with Polly and Sally. Benny was juggling, sequins from his costume flashing in the lamplight. Flossie sat hunched on the desk, picking at a bowl of gruel. John strode straight to the looking glass and started straightening his tails.

"Break a leg, Johnny," Dirk said through lips thick with maroon lipstick. He set his cigar on the edge of the ashtray to pull of the strap of his pink dress and glanced at Polly's cards.

"Damn it, Johnny!" Jackson recapped the flask and wiped his mouth.

Obadiah, bursting the seams of his coral evening gown, merely said, "Raise."

John turned away from the looking glass. "I'm ready."

As the two men jogged to the stage, Jackson gasped, "Mr. Hewes wants an extra performance tonight."

"Who this time?"

Jackson fingered the flask at his side. "Bert Dobbins."

"Run out of jokes?"

"Must've."

"And Cuddy Lane."

"Figures."

They had reached the left wing. Jackson removed the flask, and John peered into the audience. A few patrons in the balcony, none in the boxes, and a smattering of drunks on the floor. Three tables remained standing.

At the upright in the center of the stage sat Archibald Stone, slick hair parted down the middle, full mustache wet with the rye whiskey of his cocktail, paused for another sip and then launched into his final song of the evening

My key is bright, not rusty;
It is so oft applied
To locks that are not dusty
Of maidens that are lusty
And not too full with pride.

    The calliope tune rang through the theater. Jackson continued gulping until the audience broke out into applause. Archibald knocked back his drink, moved to center stage, bowed low and bowed again. Jackson shoved the flask into his pocket and dropped the curtain. The applause continued as Archibald sashayed into the wings.

    "Top that, Johnny," Archibald smirked, pushing past him to the dressing room.

    Jackson blew a raspberry and looked up at John, who felt too annoyed tonight at Archibald's arrogant pride in a tasteless performance to respond to Jackson. When the clapping died to nothing, Jackson raised the curtain. A hush spread through the crowd. John seated himself, paused a long time, and played the extended version of the piece from the Rutherford's anniversary party, the one Savannah had inspired.

    Twenty minutes later, John exited to a handful of claps. Jackson dropped the curtain. Dirk and Obadiah stood in the wings, ready to perform.

    "Better luck next time, Johnny," Dirk said.

    John was almost to the green room, with Jackson struggling to keep pace, when a voice called out, "Oh, sir!"

    Jackson stopped, astonishment on his face. "I think she means you."

    John turned. An older woman, about sixty and in full evening dress, stood before him. Her companion, a short stooped man with auburn mutton chops, thinning auburn hair, and a squint, watched John with an amused expression. In his hand was an unlit pipe, a beautiful pipe of polished dark wood and a large bowl with a gold lid, gold trim, and gold mouth piece.

    Before John could acknowledge her, the woman pushed something into his hand with a, "Please, sir, take it, sir. Your music is truly beautiful."

    "Well, I'll be a monkey's uncle! Johnny, whatcha got?"

    John opened his hand. It was a gold coin.

    "Salzburg 14 ducat," the man said. "Sixteen twelve."

    Stunned, John looked up to say, "Thank you," but the couple was gone. Jackson knocked on the green room door.

    "Come in!" Virgil yelled from the other side.

John walked in just as Jackson and Benny walked out. Still in shock, John walked to the desk to show Flossie and relate the encounter with the mysterious couple who presented it.

"See, Johnny," Flossie said, more erotic in Roman garb than Caesar ever looked, knees drawn up to her chin, smoking a cigarette, "Toldja it'd just take time."

At the far end of the room, Virgil fiddled with a demonic fury. Polly and Sally kicked up their heels and giggled as they danced, the weight of their chubby feet thump, thumping on the floor.

"I wonder who they were," John mused, as he pocketed the coin. "They didn't resemble lower Manhattan stock."

Flossie winced and drew her knees up tighter. "Want company later?"

"No."

A knock on the door. Flossie hesitated before calling out, "Come in!"

Jackson opened the door and announced, "Ten minutes, Flossie. You ready?"

Flossie glanced at John. Jackson impatiently tapped his foot.

"Yeah," Flossie crushed her cigarette. "I'm ready."

Head spinning, John dropped onto the old Windsor chair *and awakened the next morning in humbled disbelief at finding himself in Savannah's bed, awed beyond words at how she...*

The bedclothes rustled. Savannah stirred, stretched, and smiled up at him. "You're late."

"Savannah, will you marry me?"

"Marry you! Goodness, John, you're a mere..."

"I'm serious. Will you marry me?"

"I shall! Yes, John, I will."

Licking her lips, she...

"Ten minutes, Johnny! You ready?"

The door to the water closet banged open, and Obadiah's voice rang out, "Cripes jiminy, how can one gal stink so much?"

"All that gruel," Dirk said. "She eats nuttin' else."

"I'll be back. Gonna find me another hole."

A rough hand shook John's shoulder. "Johnny!"

"I'm awake," John slurred and struggled to sit.

With a half-hearted tug on his tails, John trailed after Jackson, shaking his head to clear the cobwebs and motivate it for this second performance. A handful of people had stayed, loitering by the door and talking in loud voices. Afterwards, too exhausted to reclaim his coat and hat, John climbed the fire escape stairs, scarcely noticing the garbage and sewage, broke into his room, and passed out on the bed.

It was noon before John awakened, hungry, muscles locked from not moving all night, but rested. He put on the coffee and reheated the potato soup Lila had made yesterday, while munching one of the sausages she had cooked. He sliced half a loaf, thankful for no classes or parties before tonight's show, just the opportunity to spend the rest of the day downstairs, practicing.

For several hours, John sat at the upright on the stage, until a hand closed the lid in the middle of the piece. He looked up. A man, white shirt sleeves rolled to the elbows and watch chain hanging from his sepia waistcoat stared down at him.

"Give it up, John," Dana Hewes said.

John raised the lid and resumed playing. "No."

"It's not about the practice."

"What do you suggest?"

"I suggest practice," Maestro said.

"Further practice is impossible. I doubt even you can add hours to the day."

Maestro picked up John's hand. "I see no blood. Just the soft hand of a noblewoman."

"Stuff your credentials and your outdated methods. You're merely an egotist, nothing more, nothing less."

"And you, Master John, don't want virtuosity badly enough."

"It's always about the practice."

"Go back to your society."

John laughed bitterly and stopped playing.

"I was accepted because of my father, and I'll be shunned because I humiliated my father. But whether they accept me or shun me is not the point."

Dana leaned an elbow onto the piano. "What is the point?"

"That my music touches the masses, that I build a legacy separate from my father. When my influence and affluence is greater than his, I'll go back."

"You're doing it the wrong way."

"You're firing me?"

"No, but I am suspending you for the night. Come sit in the audience with me. I'll show you what the masses want."

For several hours, John endured fire breathers, chanson singers, strip teasers, and mimes. But when Archibald Stone, slick hair parted down the middle, black overcoat and tie, and white ruffled shirt, sauntered

114

onstage and took his seat at the upright, John's patience snapped, and he started to stand. Dana put a firm hand on John's shoulder and pushed him down.

"Pay attention," Dana said.

Archibald performed song after bawdy, tasteless song, calliope tunes interspersed with sips of rye whiskey, until John thought he would vomit. The fact Archibald mesmerized the audience with vulgar comments didn't help.

"The man is coarse and profane; his music is devoid of beauty and grace," John whispered. "Why do people like it?"

Dana leaned near John's ear. "Because he makes music simple for them. They can follow it and anticipate it, so they fancy they understand it."

"I won't play ditties."

"John..."

"Only pieces that are unique, complex, and able to outlive time." Archibald's voice filled the hall.

> *He pleased her so well that backward she fell*
> *And swooned as though she were sick.*
> *So sweet was his note that up went her coat —*
> *Tis but a wanton trick.*

"I agree those are noble aspirations," Dana said. "But what difference will it make if no one hears them?"

Dana turned his attention to the stage. John said nothing, so Dana added, "Listen to me, John. No one is advising you to throw out your style and mimic Archibald Stone. His music is terrible, if you ask me."

"Why keep him?"

"Because he makes me money. Look, you don't have to abandon your work, just weave into it something people can follow. The magic is in the melody." Dana looked at John. "Have you eaten today?"

"Yes."

"Dilberries. Let's go."

But instead of heading upstairs, Dana led John outside and down the street.

"You don't live above the music hall?" John asked in surprise.

"No. One space is for my work, the other for my life. And the two should never say, 'Howdy do.'"

Dana's apartment was just a block away and nearly as drab as the music hall. Four flights of dark stairs later, Dana was unlocking a battered door and pushing it open. A saporous aroma greeted them.

"Cornish pasties," Dana said as he secured many bolts, "and snowball pudding, most delicious." He jammed a plank underneath the door knob. "Clarice!"

A tiny woman, raven hair hanging in a thick braid, eyes wide with questions, scuttled into the room and swiped glistening hands down her apron.

"Another place for dinner," Dana held up a finger, emphasized each word, and gestured to John. "One of my entertainers."

Clarice curtsied and scurried away. Except for the kitchen and another door leading to the water closet, Dana's apartment was a single large room, with a round table and four chairs at one end and a sagging brass bed at the other.

"Your housekeeper?" John asked, turning his attention back to his employer.

"My wife," Dana said, taking the chair opposite the door. "Sit and have tea with me while we wait."

Clarice soon returned with two cups and saucers, which she centered before each man before heading back to the kitchen for the teapot. Smiling, Clarice filled both cups, spilling not one drop.

"Thank you." John raised his cup, the first tea he had tasted since Spencer Inn.

She smiled shyly and left the room.

Dana took a sip. "So you won't return to Fifth Avenue?"

"Correct."

The tea had none of Mama Prudie's characteristic spices, only a touch of sugar, but it still warmed him.

"Maybe consider modifying the pieces you perform. Your music is exquisite, and I daresay even this crowd would enjoy it, if presented in a decipherable manner. Clarice!"

Clarice hurried into the room, and Dana pointed. She scurried away for the teapot and refilled Dana's cup. He pointed to John's.

"I'm fine," John said.

Clarice filled John's cup to the brim and slipped from the room. Dana grinned at John's annoyed expression, as John eyed the steaming contents.

"She can't hear you," Dana said.

"Beg pardon?"

"She's almost deaf...and mute, to boot."

"How do you communicate?"

"Through our eyes, my gestures, her service to me, and my gratefulness for it. Most men's conversation is mean and self-centered; far too many women babble about useless nonsense." Dana drew circles in the air. "We skip all that."

116

Clarice returned with a plate of dumplings for Dana and then one for John. Wondering, John cut into the mixture of chopped potatoes, turnips, onions, and minced beef. Clarice cut the bread into thick slices, spread them with large dollops of lard, and served them to Dana and John. With anxious eyes and clasped hands, Clarice waited for John to sample his pasty and nod his approval. Dana watched the exchange.

"She likes you." Dana reached for his bread as Clarice left the room.

"Isn't she eating?" John asked.

"Yes, in the kitchen. She's more comfortable there."

"Timid?"

"Not really." Dana took a quick gulp. "More due to her background. I bought her from a workhouse."

Uncertain what to comment, John continued eating. Seasoned with salt and pepper, the pasties were a little bland, but preferable to gruel.

"I needed a cheap housekeeper," Dana continued.

"But I thought you said Clarice is your..."

"She *is* my wife." Dana pushed aside his plate and settled against the chair back. "Her submission and willingness to care for my every need endeared her to me. So, I married her."

Meal complete, Clarice removed the plates and brought out cream, sugar, two saucers. Standing upright in each saucer was a baked apple. Dana sprinkled sugar on his and then poured cream over it, so John did the same and slid his spoon inside. The filling was cooked rice.

"So, John, do we have an understanding?"

"I don't know."

The next morning, John hailed a cab and headed for M. Harrington & Sons to have the ducat appraised. He couldn't wait to see the expression on Marshall's face when he saw the rare coin.

"Mr. Harrington is very busy," the clerk said, inspecting John's attire with a critical eye, obviously doubting John's claim of knowing Marshall well.

"He'll make time to see this."

He removed his wallet to show the clerk the ducat, eager to see the clerk's eyes pop. Instead, John's popped. The ducat was gone.

"See what?" the clerk asked impatiently.

Reeling from this blow, John stumbled out of the bank and trudged to Central Park, where he spent the night and the following day wandering the grounds, thinking. Compromise went against everything inside him, but crawling back to his father's home as a music hall failure, broken and defeated with no shelter save for his lunatic mother's arms, was inconceivable. He'd die first.

About midnight, John spied a partial loaf in a trash barrel. He brushed away the slugs and devoured it, not the least ashamed that the son of Farlow Abbot Simons was feasting on garbage so close to his childhood home. Exhausted, stomach churning, he stretched out next to the barrel, studied his star, and tried to think through a mind of mush.

"The magic is in the melody," John mumbled, closing his eyes, ignoring the hunger, and drifting away.

CHAPTER EIGHT: ONE FOR THE MEMORY BOOKS

It took over five years, but John's feverish reworking of elaborate compositions to include melodic refrains and then monitoring audience response to the changes and rewriting pieces after midnight for the next day's practice based on responses, finally produced results.

Gradually, but steadily, John's traffic grew, and so did the popularity of Hewes Music Hall, cementing John's employment and increasing his wages. When the weekend crowd began attracting some upper Manhattan folks, John became the highest paid performer, and he let the teaching go. Then came the night Archibald Stone was a no-show, and John never saw him again. Dana gave John Archibald's private dressing room, which was hardly private, as John shared the space with a colony of water bugs.

The only blight on John's happiness was Falconer Cremmins. Last year, Dana had invited this bossy man with squinting eyes and a nasty temper to become a junior partner. Although the performers rarely saw Falconer, they felt the results of his growing influence.

One breezy day in May eighteen eighty-eight, Dana, carrying a maroon top hat, interrupted John's practice to introduce him to a young man: short, slim, wavy brown hair brushing his shoulders, tailored maroon suit and matching overcoat and pink ruffled shirt.

"John," Dana said. "This is a reporter from the New York Gazette. He's writing a story about my establishment and wants to ask you a few questions."

The dandy extended a gloved hand, the one not holding the black-bound notebook and ivory propelling pencil. "Henry Matthews."

Slowly John rose as he warily returned the greeting. "John Simons."

Henry opened his notebook. "The banker's son?"

"Yes."

Henry gestured to the piano with his pencil. "All original compositions?"

"Yes."

"Care to play a sample?"

"No."

"Perform daily?"

"Except Sundays."

"How long?"

"Five years."

The pencil-scratching stopped. Henry raised an eyebrow and looked John up and down, from the worn shoes to the mane of snarled hair. "Sole income source?"

"Presently."

"Previously?"

"Some supplementation."

"By?"

"Tutoring, parlor parties."

"Goals?"

Silence.

"Tell me, John," Henry said with a flourish of his pencil, "has the minimal slum following you've developed been worth the loss of gold in the till and Daddy's connections?"

"*No* comment."

"What time do you appear tonight?"

"Why all the questions?"

"Nine o'clock," Dana said.

Henry grinned as he slapped the notebook shut. "I like to be thorough." He turned to Dana and shook his hand with a dip of his head. "Much obliged for your time."

"Would you care to speak with my partner, Mr. Falconer Cremmins?"

"No need. I've all the information I require."

"Well, then." Dana handed Henry his hat. "I'll walk you to the door."

"It's possible Mr. Burroughs will attend this evening's show and take some photographs for..." Henry's voice faded away as the two men left the theater.

John was halfway through a rhapsody when Dana crossed the stage and into the left wing. John immediately stopped playing and followed Dana back to the dressing rooms.

"I don't trust him," John said. "He's not a typical journalist."

"Good insight."

"Meaning?"

"Meaning there's not a whit of commonality about Henry Matthews. He's engaged to Agnes King, and he's Lord Girard's ward and heir."

Taken aback at the unexpected regality of the news, and the fact someone like Dana Hewes knew of Lord Girard, John said as casually as he could, "My point. Why is someone that wealthy working for the Gazette?"

"I'm sure it's simple formality. Lord Girard owns the Gazette."

"He...he does?"

Dana stopped short and looked at John with astonishment and skepticism. John's feigned surprised hadn't fooled him.

"But," John hastily added, "given His Lordship's reach, I'm not surprised."

They'd reached the back of the theater.

"I'm heading home for dinner," Dana turned to John. The expression in his eyes, almost kind. "Join me?"

"Not tonight, but thank you."

John returned to the piano, but memory of that afternoon's interview, as well as Dana's knowledge, plagued him. After one stupid mistake after another, John reluctantly shut the lid, annoyed for allowing a pretentious dandy to interfere with his music, employed (most likely) because the man's guardian had commodities and influence. Henry probably couldn't write worth a damn, and Dana probably didn't know Lord Girard or anyone close to him. Dana probably overheard it from a drunk customer.

John was still brooding later that night when Jackson knocked on his dressing room door.

"Ten minutes, Johnny. Ready?"

"Almost."

John hurried to the green room to check his appearance, the only room in the music hall with a looking glass. As he straightened his tails, he saw Benny drop a ball, Virgil stop fiddling to find it, and Jackson gulp long and hard from his flask.

"Break a leg, Johnny," Dirk said, peering at Polly's cards and handing Sally a cigar.

Obadiah merely said, "Raise."

As John and Jackson trotted toward the stage, Jackson said, "Mr. Hewes wants an extra performance tonight."

"Who's the no-show this time?"

"Cuddy Lane, and he's not a no-show. Mr. Cremmins done fired him."

"Long overdue."

"Agreed."

They had reached the left wing. John peered into the auditorium. The balconies, boxes and main floor were packed, and only about half of the patrons appeared drunk. Some were standing and shouting to their companions over the din; others were actually listening to the minstrel show. Jackson took another swig and wiped his mouth on his grimy coat sleeve, leaving a line of soot across his upper lip. John shuffled restlessly and waited for the applause that would signal the start of his appearance.

As the actors filed off the stage, Jackson dropped the curtain, and John strode to the upright, settling himself, pausing, and waiting for the curtain to rise. An hour later, John strutted off the stage to thunderous applause and the awe of Dirk and Obadiah, waiting in the wings, ready to perform.

"Atta boy, Johnny!" Dirk exclaimed, vigorously nodding, pig tails swinging.

John had nearly reached the green room when a panting Jackson caught up to him.

"Audience sure 'ppreciates good music!"

John said nothing. Jackson rapped on the door. Virgil called out, "Come in!" After a quick gulp, Jackson flung open the door. "Ten minutes, Benny. You ready?"

The juggler straightened his leotards and then reached for his bag.

"Urry," Jackson replaced the cap and nodded to John. "Up again in an hour."

Jackson shut the door behind them.

"You wowed them agin, Johnny," Flossie McGee said, smoking a cigarette from her perch on the desk, knees drawn up to her chin. "We could hear their admiration."

Bert Dobbins peered over yesterday's edition of the New York Gazette, eyes flitting over Flossie's regency wig, breeches, tall boots, and brass-buckled coat.

"Never you mind, Flossie," Bert said with a wink. "Dere's plenty to admire right back 'ere."

In seconds, John had ripped the newspaper from Bert's hands and was grabbing Bert by the throat. "Apologize."

Flossie blinked, winced, and drew her knees up tighter. Virgil stopped fiddling.

"Hey, now, Johnny, ya lettin' success go to yer..." Bert began, the fright on his face contradicting his bold words.

John's fingers tightened. Bert gagged and coughed.

"Johnny, let 'im go," Flossie protested. "I'm sure he didn't mean nuttin'..."

"Sorry," Bert spluttered.

John released his hold and dropped into the Windsor chair. Bert jumped to his feet and ran from the green room, hollering for Jackson.

Flossie snuffed out the cigarette and looked at John. "I'm goin' out. Jackson might be too busy to git me in time."

Exhausted, John closed his eyes, but a light touch on his arm made him quickly reopen them. Flossie's face was gray and the lines around her mouth were hard, despite the heavy stage makeup.

"Thanks, Johnny," she whispered.

John closed his eyes and *galloped across the countryside, lush and green in its summer glory, only stopping to rest the horses near a brook and kneel beside babbling waters to drink. Face dripping, Savannah*

122

stretched out in the grass and then reached up to tweak his cheek.

Without thinking, he caught her finger between his teeth and held it. Savannah grinned and wriggled in delight and anticipation. John moved down and then farther down until he tasted something better than blackberries...

"Stay away from the loo," Obadiah called in the far distance, "Flossie was in there."

A door closed; another banged open.

"Ten minutes, Johnny!"

"Damn it, I know!"

After playing to an overflowing house, John dragged himself back to the empty dressing room, retrieved his top hat and coat, and then trudged up the fire escape stairs, the stench of garbage and sewage surrounding him all the way. At least he still had his star. He forced up the window and passed out on the bed the moment he lowered the sash.

Earsplitting thunder woke John the next morning. A blinding flash, then blackness. He pulled back the curtain. Sheets of rain pelted his window. Cramped from sleeping in one position, John rolled out of bed with a groan and staggered to the stove to start the coffee and scramble some eggs, the latter a morning staple now that John was earning more money. When the toast was brown and crisp, John sat down to breakfast and mentally listed the pieces he would rehearse. He had just poured another cup of coffee when he glanced at the wall clock. Half past ten! How had he...?

It was the storm, John thought, as he hurriedly splashed water over his face, the storm and his fatigue. He hastened into his clothes and dashed downstairs. Five minutes into his first selection, he heard Jackson yelling, "Johnny, hey Johnny!"

Fingers prancing across the keys and vexed at the interruption, John glanced over his shoulder. Jackson was speeding toward him, waving a newspaper.

"Hey, Johnny, look!" Bracing himself on his knees, gasping, face damp, Jackson held up the New York Gazette. "You made the front page of the morning edition!"

Stunned, John snatched the newspaper, noted the large photo of him at the upright, and read:

Estranged son of Fifth Avenue banker regales music-hall goers

Hewes Music Hall in Lower Manhattan is the perfect venue for that touch of English vaudeville, no doubt because the founder and co-owner, Dana Hewes, is, in fact, English.

But it's not the minstrels and the mimes who are drawing crowds and keeping them inside. It's John Simons, son of no other than Farlow Abbot Simons, president of F.A. Simons and Company.

The younger Simons, a pianist of incomparable talent and unlike anything New York City has ever experienced, unceasingly played his original compositions for one hour, although so bewitching was the music it seemed but seconds.

According to Hewes, Simons is the protégé of master pianist Seymour Cassidy (deceased), who tutored Simons during his boyhood. At 14, Simons became the youngest pupil to enter Wesley Music Conservatory in Connecticut, graduating at the top of his class and refusing a salaried teaching position in favor of performance, Hewes also said.

Realizing Simons' musical genius, Hewes hired Simons on the spot and eventually gave Simons top billing. Before that time, Simons graciously shared his talent in the form of private piano lessons and in-home parties.

Except Sundays, when Hewes Music Hall is closed in honor of the Lord's Day, Simons can be heard every evening at 9 p.m. He's mum about his goals, which could be attributed to modesty rather than lack of direction, as Cassidy's influence is strong in Simons' music, but without mimicry.

Simons has his own style: complicated, yet melodic; smooth, but exciting; enchanting as well as overpowering in a way that satisfies both the ears and the eyes.

The eyes, you ask?

A John Simons concert is as pleasing visually as it is audibly. Donned in lavish white tails, Simons' posture is tall and proud, the finger movements confident and exact, the expression a mystery, whether he is playing a sonata, a rhapsody, or a dirge. Trust me, Simons doesn't disappoint and is worth every bit of the $2 entrance fee...

"You done, Johnny? I wanna show Mr. Hewes."

In a daze, John gave the newspaper back to Jackson, who sped away as though wild boars were chasing him. John hesitated, but not for long. He closed the piano lid, dashed outside, and hailed cab.

"Where to?" the driver asked.

"Nassau Street."

"Straight away, sir."

The New York Gazette made its home on the second floor of a five-story building with a cast-iron facade. The newsroom itself was roomy and noisy, full of men in waistcoats and high collars clacking away on typewriters.

"May I help you, sir?"

124

John gazed down at the young clerk sitting behind the large front desk. "I'm looking for Henry Matthews."

"He's on assignment.," the clerk said, dipping his pen and opening a ruled book. "I can take a message."

"I'll wait."

"Sir, he could be gone for..."

"I said, 'I'll wait.' Mind if I look at this?"

John pointed to a copy of that morning's edition.

"Not at all," the clerk said.

So John settled into a chair and proceeded to read the rest. Henry had spoken the truth. He was indeed thorough. With quotes from Oliver Dorchester, Hugh Blanchard, Mortimer Rutherford, Dana Hewes, and a few others John did not recognize, (most likely associates of his father's due to the scathing comments they made about Abbott's disregard for John's music), the story detailed John's musical back story, from the impromptu drawing room concert when John was eleven, to the tutelage of Maestro Seymour Cassidy, his audition into Wesley Music Conservatory and refusal of a teaching post, and to his present day performances at Hewes Music Hall.

"Who could have imagined one would find such exquisite talent in lower Manhattan," Henry had written.

An hour, then two, and then three passed before Henry, in navy overcoat, top hat and cravat appeared. If he seemed surprised to see John, he didn't show it.

"Thank you for the story," John said, rising and offering his hand, "and I apologize for my earlier rudeness."

"Accepted," Henry said with a hearty handshake of his own. "I'm famished. Delmonico's? My treat."

"I couldn't, but..."

"Nonsense. It's just the corner. You'll be back at the music hall in plenty of time. Give me a moment to pop into Mr. McCloud's office, and we'll be on our way." He nodded his head to the Gazette next to John's chair. "You may keep the copy."

John knew Delmonico's location and missing show time was not his objection, but he couldn't very well argue with Henry in the middle of the newsroom, especially since he had his own questions for Henry. So he returned to his chair while Henry disappeared into the office. Ten minutes later, Henry was strolling back out, pulling on his gloves and approaching the clerk.

"I shan't return until morning," Henry said. "I have an engagement this evening."

"Noted, Mr. Matthews," the clerk said, entering the message into the notebook. "Have a good night."

John had not dined at Delmonico's since the week before Emily King's debutante ball, shortly before leaving for New Haven to work for Savannah. It felt surreal to be so close to his boyhood home, sitting with a reporter related to someone within his father's business circle, and casually ordering premium steak instead of eating half-spoiled food. The waiter had scarcely scurried away with their orders when John took a sip of the sangaree and sprung it on Henry.

"How did you glean my style from a short burst of questions?"

"I didn't," Henry's eyes twinkled as he tasted his own drink. "I was in the audience last night."

"You never mentioned that was your plan."

"It wasn't my plan," Henry coolly returned. "And you didn't ask."

"Then may I question you now?"

"Certainly."

John hesitated. He could leave and pretend none of this occurred. He could return to Hewes Music Hall, thankful for the publicity and simply continue along his path. The dandy held his glass in the air, expectantly awaiting John's interrogation, while John fumbled with the growing notion that this intersection of their lives might very well be God's will.

John started easy. "Are you from New York?"

"No, I'm a recent resident, originally from Chicago."

"So you didn't grow up in Lord Girard's household?"

"I didn't say that."

"Please elaborate."

Henry grinned. "Don't glance back, move forward, I always say." He took a sip, not once breaking his gaze. "Next question."

The waiter returned. "Another drink?"

"Yes," Henry nodded toward John, "For me and my comrade."

John studied the other tables until the waiter left and then asked, "You're engaged to Agnes King?"

"I am."

Savannah climbed to her knees and threw her arms around John's neck. "Mrs. John Simons. I can't wait!"

Henry serenely waited for the next question. His features divulged nothing of Cupid's spell.

"You're in love with Agnes?"

"I'm in love with her money."

"A pity she had a conflict, but I suppose she must be quite busy with finances. Mr. Holloway had amassed a substantial fortune."

"My interest is Savannah, not her money."

"Her money? Won't you inherit Lord Girard's estate when he dies?

Henry shrugged. "One never has too much money."

John thoughtfully sipped his wine and considered his father, then this Henry Matthews, rich by birth and intending to be rich by marriage, too. He recalled the long sermons of Father McClosky, who had preached that the love of money was the root of all evil.

"Look, Agnes and I get on jolly well," Henry said, "Isn't that sufficient grounds for marriage?"

The waiter returned with their steaks. Henry picked up his knife and fork and deftly changed the subject.

"So John, tell me how you made Seymour Cassidy's acquaintance."

That night, still keyed up from front page notoriety and still pondering the advantages and disadvantages of an alliance with Henry Matthews, John pushed aside the covers, swung his legs over the edge of the bed, and reached under his pillow for his wallet. Opening it, he removed and contemplated, one by one, those calling cards he had collected from the Rutherfords' anniversary party. Beside him, Flossie stirred, rolled onto her side, and propped herself up.

"Watcha got there, Johnny?"

"Good luck charms. See?"

John set them by her, but Flossie shook her head.

"Them's too good for the likes of me, Johnny."

"Just read them."

Flossie hesitated. Even in the dim light, John noticed her sad face.

"I can't read, Johnny."

John picked up the cards. "Then I will read them for you." And John did.

Herbert Rutherford

Marshall Harrington

Albert Brumfeldt

Bartholomew Smythe.

Before John could finish, Flossie reached up to stroke his cheek. "Why keep them, when they make you sad?"

Abruptly, John shoved the cards back in his wallet and lay down, clasping his hands behind his neck and staring at the ceiling.

"One day, Flossie, those people will beg for my presence." His voice was low and dark. "The cards are visible reminders of it."

Flossie burrowed into his side and stroked his bare chest.

"You're better'n rest of us, Johnny," she said sleepily. "You're gonna make it."

Ticket sales remained high for days, and John inwardly rejoiced, for March's terrible blizzard, and the flooding that followed, affected business for weeks. One afternoon, as John launched into his final practice piece, Henry walked up to him.

"I dying to try McSorley's. Shall we?"

They took a cab to lower Manhattan, with Henry chatting all the way about New York's cantankerous weather and how it kept him busy with news articles even as it ruined one suit after another. Despite Henry's fine manners, he seemed equally at home with the rustic McSorley's as he had been inside Delmonico's.

Not until John picked up his ale and took a long drink, the type of drink Jackson would approve, did he dare ask, "So Lord Girard's ward enjoys reporting?"

"I never said I enjoyed it." Henry raised his glass to his lips and sipped it. "Well, this is quite good."

"Writing is not your passion?" John couldn't fathom why anyone as rich as Henry was would engage in business he did not enjoy, especially when he need not engage in business at all.

"Journalism is not my passion," Henry set down his glass. "But writing most certainly is, the main reason for my marriage to Agnes King."

"I don't understand."

Henry held out the plate. "Soda cracker?"

John shook his head, still watching Henry.

"I prefer shocking to informing." Henry grabbed another cracker. "Supernatural stories, not news stories.

"I see."

"But penning content for dime novels doesn't pay Fifth Avenue rent."

"You're renting? On Fifth Avenue? But I thought..."

"That I subsisted off Lord Girard's riches? Hardly."

"And a reporter's salary covers those expenses?"

Amusement on his lips. Henry took out a card, inscribed something on it, and then passed it to John. "This is my address. You're welcome to call on me."

128

John read the card. His eyes widened. Henry merely cut another slice of turkey and said, "I see you recognize the address. My, did Mr. Russell have plenty to say about you when my story broke."

"About?"

"About how Little Lonnie, who's not quite so little anymore, would be so accomplished if you hadn't abandoned your commitment to teaching 'the dear one.'"

Henry, John thought, for all his dandyisms, understood more than he showed.

"So," John said, deciding no further remarks about the Russells were necessary. "You intend to use the King family riches to further your goals?"

"Not exactly, no. I view it as an exchange of resources. Trust me, Agnes King is, and will be, amply compensated."

"I still don't comprehend why you must marry Agnes when you have Lord Girard as a...resource."

Henry waved for the bill and then leaned forward with a sly look.

"Lord Girard is fairly young and healthy, making an early demise and acquisition of his inheritance unlikely for some time."

"That's cold."

"See here, John, don't act so coy. You and I, we are nearly the same."

"How so?"

"Similar resources, congruent goals, but..." Henry grinned impishly. "... different applications."

John said nothing.

Henry leaned back and winked. "Would you like an invitation to play for one of Mr. King's parties?"

"Go back to the society that accepts you."

"I was accepted because of my father, and I'll be shunned because I humiliated my father. But whether they accept me or shun me is not the point."

Dana leaned an elbow onto the piano and looked intently at John. "What is the point?"

"That my music touch the masses, that I build my own legacy separate from that of my father's. When my influence is greater than his, then I'll go back."

Henry raised an expectant eyebrow. But Henry had also said one should move forward and not glance back.

"I'll let you know," John said.

Over the next few weeks, Henry's appearances at the music hall increased in frequency, as did his and John's meals together. Nevertheless, the more time John spent in Henry's company, the more jealous he became of Henry's situation.

How easily Henry could switch off his conscience in order to use other people's wealth for his own purposes, despite the fact that Lord Girard seemed overall supportive of Henry's abilities in pursuits. At the very least, Henry's aspirations did not oppose His Lordship's wishes, as John's had with Abbott's.

And yet, he felt a connection to Henry, perplexing since John felt connected to few people. He began meeting Henry at Crook & Duff's new location at 16 Park Place for broiled oysters and corned beef hash. They lingered so long at dinner one night that a frantic Jackson ran into John as he entered the backstage.

"Where ya been, Johnny?" Jackson reached for his flask. "Dana's home with the grippe and Mr. Cremmins is ranting like a lunatic."

"Cremmins can go to hell."

"He's demanding an extra performance from you tonight."

"And the no-show this time?"

"Flossie McGee."

John spun around and sprinted for the exit.

"Hey, watcha doin'?" Jackson's indignant shouting followed John out the door. "Mr. Cremmins ain't gonna like it!"

John sped down 11th Street, weaving through the alleys and pushing aside anyone in his way. Although John had never visited Flossie's lodgings, he knew where she lived, and he soon reached the building, a dilapidated shack behind a row of tenements, poorly constructed from whatever materials could be carried from the unofficial dump down the street.

He flew up the rickety steps, burst inside, stepped into garbage up to his ankles. Two elderly women crouched near a fire in a garbage barrel, warming their hands. One man was passed out in the corner. Guarding him was an emaciated mutt, head on his paws, alternately growling and whining.

"Where's Flossie?" John asked of a disheveled man, audaciously smoking one of the Haunch's cigarettes and peering up at John from beneath the wide brim of his floppy hat.

The man pointed to the back of the room and then had the gall to ask, "Got any more fags?"

John ducked beneath the sagging roof, and there lay Flossie on an old feather bed under a broken beam, her face the color of classroom chalk, dilated pupils staring at nothing, coverlets soaked in blood. John could only gape, eyes stinging, heart pounding, breaths coming in strangled gasps.

Sorry, Johnny," the man called out. "Damned gastritis finally gotter."

Blindly, John stumbled out of the building and groped his way down the stairs. A mournful groan caused him to uncontrollably tremble and miss two steps until John realized he was making the noise. No more. *No more! NO FUCKING MORE!*

John ran until he reached Methodist Episcopal Church where Helsby and Felicity were married. It was open, so John went inside, knelt in the back pew, and said a prayer for the salvation of her soul, as well as his.

Once again outside, John hailed a cab and quickly rattled off the address. As it pulled into the dark street, now sparse with traffic, John rehearsed his speech, including his reasons for delay and why he now felt ready to perform for the Kings. New York's underbelly be damned, where beautiful, talented, courageous, *good* girls...

He closed his eyes and held his breath. *No more.*

The sky was absent of light, save for his star, the only one that mattered. Yet, when John reached Fifth Avenue and banged and shouted outside that mansion door, until a sleepy maid finally answered it, John had another shock.

"Oh Henry's gone," the maid said, yawning, swaying, and blinking against sleep, "to London, for the season."

"I didn't know," John stammered, backing away. So soon? They just had dinner. "Thank you."

Staggering under that blow, John counted his dwindling money, and again hailed a cab. He huddled into the seat for the dismal trip to Lower Manhattan, thankful Henry would never know this squelching of pride and kicking himself for not sooner befriending Lord Girard's golden charge. In a twinkling, his romance with music halls had become a quicksand of despair, dragging John down, down, down, down, down, down, down, down, down,

down,

down,

down,

down into crackling tongues; and melting flesh; and writhing wisps; and shrieking shadows snapping like lion trainers' whips; and dazzling flames leaping, pirouetting, and chasing their tails with mad frenzy, while in the inferno's center sat Satan, regal and unscathed, hair swept off his forehead and tangled in his thick horns, gray-blond strands sticking to his unlined face, as he tossed back his head and roared, "MUAHAHAHAHHAHAHAHAHAHAHAHAHAHAHAHAHA!" The air sizzled and snapped; orange tongues split an angry red sky; and the horses screamed and frantically lurched.

"Holy Mother of God!" the cab driver shouted.

John's eyes fluttered open in time to see the flaming floors of Dana and Clarice's apartment building collapse into glowing ash.

CHAPTER NINE: THE CONTRACT

Although Falconer Cremmins was a hard man, and possibly a conniving murderous one, as unproven rumors of arson spread throughout Queens, he also proved to be witless at business. In the year after Dana Hewes' death, attendance steadily dwindled at the music hall until Cremmins was forced to close its doors.

Disgusted at himself for nearly caving into Henry's invitation to play for the Kings, John redoubled his efforts towards his own notoriety, without his father's connections to shorten the process. But Cremmins' mismanagement of the music hall, coupled with the man's sleazy reputation, blackened the public's perception of the performers, too, so John found himself unable to book even parlor parties to supplement his fading wages. Many times, when John went to pay the rent, he found it already paid, which he attributed to Henry, who still occasionally met with John for dinner.

But when April reappeared, and Henry again departed for London with the Kings, John realized his supplementary income had also left, at least until September, when Henry would return to New York City, if John lived that long. For the last month, in order to stretch the little money he had left, John had subsisted on a single porridge meal a day.

Thus John mused as he stood in the empty dressing room and donned his white tails for his final performance, ignoring the hunger in his belly and the buzzing in his head. He had little money left; the rent was due; and he had no further engagements scheduled. John had often wondered how he might react should this day arrive. Now that it had, John accepted his fate with an eerie serenity. He had vowed to play or die; he just might get the latter. One day, someone would find him dead in his bed, much as he had discovered Flossie. But what did it matter? He had played, and he had played on his own terms. Wearily, John combed his hair and then headed downstairs, his spirits as dreary as the gray twilight, his heart as heavy as the fog swirling past the windows.

The mood inside the green room matched the gloom outside. Benny sat on the desk, absently tossing a ball from one hand to another and staring at nothing. Virgil tuned his fiddle. Dirk leaned against the wall in a torn and stained sapphire gown, smoking a cigar and holding a second lit one in his other hand. All the can-can girls had quit long ago and taken the playing cards with them. Obadiah was nowhere in sight. An unconscious sigh escaped John's lips as he settled into the Windsor chair.

Benny set the ball between his legs and looked at John. "Ever thought it would end like this?"

"No."

Despite the rumblings in his stomach, John's mind drifted to last night's cawing, weaving through dreams of shades and massive crows, evil in their coffee-colored eyes...

Bang!

Obadiah stumbled out of the water closet, face sweating, panting. Dirk handed Obadiah the second cigar, who gratefully accepted it as he collapsed onto the settee.

"Poker?" Obadiah asked no one in particular.

Virgil replied with an off-key twang-twang. The green room door pushed open.

"Ten minutes, Johnny," Jackson slurred, replacing his flask. "Ready?"

"Sure."

Dirk kept his eyes on the floor. "Break a leg, Johnny."

After a quick check of his appearance in the looking glass, John plodded to main part of the house, with Jackson repeatedly ordering him to "'urry" and not telling him Mr. Cremmins wanted an extra performance tonight.

They had reached the left wing. John peered into the auditorium. Balconies: empty; boxes: empty; main floor: nearly empty, and those patrons on the floor were too drunk to notice the skit nearing its end onstage. Jackson emptied his flask and then dropped the curtain. As the actors clomped into the wings, John walked to the upright and waited for the curtain to rise. An hour later, John exited to a handful of lackluster claps. Dirk and Obadiah waited like condemned men at the gallows.

John held out his hand. "Gentlemen, it's been a pleasure."

Dirk, and then Obadiah, limply returned the shake.

"Likewise," Dirk said tonelessly.

"Ditto," Obadiah echoed.

"Move!" Jackson hissed at the pantomime dames, and, then, with a glare at John, "Yer holdin' up the show!"

That was Jackson, loyal to the end. Dana Hewes would be proud. Without another word, John trudged down the dark and silent back of the house to the dressing room, retrieved his coat and hat, and exited through the rear door. Much of the fog had dissipated and appeared to be moving east, as the air was clear to John's left and steamy to his right. As he started for the staircase, a fleeting movement caught his eye, a dark wisp and then nothing. A drunk pillaging the trash barrels for a midnight sack? A thief waiting to accost him? Motionless, John waited. He heard nothing except his own breaths and the drumming of his heart. He set foot on the first stair, and a silhouette slipped through the haze.

"Who is it?" John called out.

A pair of red eyes stared back. A form took shape in the gloom. Out stepped a man, his sleek hair and goatee blacker than his top hat and cloak.

"I am the devil," the stranger replied with a faint German accent.

He was simply an eccentric and John had met plenty of that type during these last years. With a tip of his hat, John sarcastically said, "A pleasant evening to you, sir," and turned toward the fire escape, but the stranger was now walking down the stairs in John's direction and examining him with a studious air. John stopped short, wondering how the man had moved so quickly, until the stranger stood before him, leaned closed, and sniffed his neck.

"Do you not fear me?" the stranger murmured, his gaze flitting over John's face.

"No."

"My very sight doesn't chill your blood?"

John attempted to move past, but the stranger grasped the rail, barring John's way. "Mr. Simons, do you know who I am?"

"No and don't really care."

"I..." The stranger raised a finger and passed it back and forth across John's face, "I am a well-connected concert promoter, well-acquainted with your exquisite musical reputation."

This time, John took a step back, the better to examine this man: deathly pallor, swarthy hollow eyes, crimson lips, and sharp white teeth.

"Is that a fact?"

"Ohhh, yes, indeed, Mr. Simons. Would you dine with me this enchanted evening?"

Ravenous and still unafraid, John nevertheless paused. Was this man as strange and sinister as he appeared, or had days of insufficient food blunted his judgment and clouded his perception? Apparently, the stranger mistook John's silence for assent, for he swept out his arm in the direction of the alley and said, "Step this way, Mr. Simons."

The man proceeded down the passageway, and John, not quite understanding why, followed him. As they moved away from the music hall, the fog grew heavier, and the buildings faded into the brume. John kept close pace with shadow ahead of him. Visibility was nil, and it toyed with his weary and sluggish mind. It seemed to John as if they had walked miles, before the fog stretched into wisps, and the scene emerged. Not one building looked familiar. John shook his head, hoping to restore clarity, as he followed the man into a three-story building and to a table at the back of the dark and bustling dining room, far too busy for the night's wee hours.

The stranger slouched against the wall, humming a little tune, smiling at nothing in particular, and drumming his fingers on the white cloth. John's head swam. A loud snap brought him back to reality and to a table full of food: roasted meats, potatoes swimming in butter, creamed vegetables, puddings of every kind, several loaves of bread, and a covered tureen.

At first, John ate with composure, but hunger soon overpowered him. As John stuffed his mouth with chunks of bread; drained glass after glass of wine; devoured the chicken and the beef; and took serving after serving of creamed vegetables, turtle soup and an assortment of puddings, John noticed his host did not partake.

"I've already feasted." the stranger said, reaching for the ladle and refilling John's bowl.

John stopped chewing. He had not voiced his observation aloud. He swallowed, slowly, and reached for the goblet.

The stranger leaned forward and dropped his voice. "Mr. Simons, how would you like to be the premiere musical artist throughout all western civilization?'

"Like it?" John choked on the wine. "I'd die for it."

"Hee, hee, hee." His eyes blazed, he stroked his goatee. "Rest assured. Those terms are not in my contract.

Wary now, John pushed away his plate and peered closely at his host. "Who are you?"

The stranger grinned with fiendish delight. "I'm a vampire, eager to barter."

Despite his fatigue, John was on his feet in seconds, hat and coat in hand.

"You're mad." John said as calmly as shaking voice allowed. "But thank you for dinner."

"Insane, am I?" With a snap of his fingers, the stranger pointed around the room. "Examine your surroundings, Mr. Simons. Do you still accuse me?"

John glanced around the room. It was now packed wall to wall with women wearing Brunswick gowns and men in short waistcoats, knee-length breeches, and tricorne hats, a perfect setting for a Colonial painting in one of Helsby's history books.

Slowly, John sat back down. He should have gone straight to his room. Or maybe he had reached the garret and was now in the throes of a nightmare. Maybe he had died outside the theater and had wound up in hell.

John glanced at his leering companion. Maybe.

"What do you want?"

"Oh, Mr. Simons, I want the very thing you want."

"You want my success?" John asked, doubting that's what this man could mean.

"Your worldwide success."

"What do you get from it?"

The man clicked his tongue, tilted his head, and smiled. "Your blood."

John's heart began to pound. "No deal."

"Oh, Mr. Simons, not all your blood. Just samples..." The man waved his hand in the air, "from time to time."

"Vampires don't...sample."

"If I drained your blood, you'd die." At these words, the stranger's eyes gleamed like coal. "And then I couldn't drink again and again and again..."

The stranger licked his lips with a contented moan and became lost in a private revelry. In a few moments, he sat straight and then said, "No, Mr. Simons, I'm telling the truth. I would never empty your veins of blood. I only desire occasional sips."

"Why?"

"Let's just say," and here the stranger tittered. "Let's just say I have a taste for musicians." He leaned across the table and pressed his lips to John's ear. "I do come with references of gratified clients." His voice was hushed, but malevolent.

"No," John said, feeling his resolve slip.

"Oh, and," the stranger, still whispering, patted John's cheek. "And a free trial."

"A free...trial?"

"Three successful concerts in the venues of your choice, anywhere in the world." He patted John's other cheek. "If you're pleased, we seal our contract in blood." His voice was barely audible, but stern; his half-mast eyes were dreamy. "Your blood."

John glanced away, but the stranger's fingertips drew John's face back. "If you're dissatisfied with the results, I won't bind you."

"Three concerts?"

The stranger gripped John's cheeks. "Yes, Mr. Simons.

"Venues of my choice?"

"Yeeeeeees, Mr. Simons."

"Successful concerts?"

The man let John go and batted his lashes. "Bargain struck?"

"I'll let you know, after the three concerts."

To John's surprise, he found himself standing on the fire escape stairs.

"Fair enough," the stranger said, continuing down the steps. "I'll return when you're ready to schedule the first one."

John whirled around. The man had already reached the ground and was hurrying across the street.

"Mr. Vampire?"

The stranger spun on his heel and faced John. "Yes?"

"Do you have a name?"

"Naturally," the stranger said with an exaggerated bow. "I'm Kellen, Kellen Wechsler."

With that, the man dissipated like steam. Bewildered, John turned and slowly climbed to the garret. He thought of Faust, madmen who consumed men's blood while they slept, Granny Spencer and her garden, Eastern European vampire legends, and Henry's words: *You and I, we are nearly the same...similar resources, congruent goals, but different applications.* Would trading small amounts of blood for worldwide fame be any different than marrying into the King family for the leisure of writing sensational fiction?

John shook his head against these preposterous thoughts and briefly entertained the notion he had been dreaming, except indigestion spoke otherwise. With a full mind and a stomach churning from an abundance of excellent food, John pushed open the window and rolled onto his bed.

CHAPTER TEN: CROSSING THE RUBICON

Shivering, John pulled the musty quilt over his head, but instead of soothing him back into sleep, the pattering rain reminded him he had drunk far too much, far too many hours ago. With a groan, John kicked off the covers and staggered down hall to the communal water closet.

Even before he pushed open the garret door on the return trip, John smelled pepper, maple sugar, and coffee. He entered, blinked, and then rubbed his gritty eyes, but the vision remained. His table was covered in ivory damask and filled with platters of sausage, flannel cakes dripping with pear butter, a steaming stainless steel coffee pot. The scene featured just one place setting, made of Spode China with a very familiar blue and white floral pattern.

A man presided over the repast, one dressed in black from head to toe and whose ashen face accentuated his coal-black eyes, hair, and goatee. The lapel held a fragrant red rose.

"I brought breakfast," Kellen said.

In a daze, John relocked and bolted the door. Who was this man? A hypnotist? A magician?

"Spencer Inn, eighteen fifty-nine," Kellen replied with a self-satisfied smirk as he stroked his chin. "Your Mama Prudie and the girls were done serving, so I helped myself to leftovers."

"Aren't you supposed to rise from the grave only at night?"

"Eastern European legends do such injustice." Kellen gestured at the food. "Sit. Eat. Oh, the trouble I endured to bring it for you."

The many days of meager food overruled John's suspicions. With one eye on Kellen, John seated himself at the table. Slowly, John ate; steadily, Kellen watched. Every bite tasted exactly as he remembered. Meanwhile, rain pattered onto the fire escape and trickled down the window.

"Nothing for you?" John said, breaking the silence as he refilled his cup, lingering on the pot's warmth in the damp room. "Or do you adhere to a strict blood-sucking diet?"

"I've dined."

"On whom?"

With a mocking sigh and roll of his eyes, Kellen popped a sausage patty into his mouth, chewed with exaggeration, swallowed with a large gulp, and then opened wide enough for John to see his tonsils. "Satisfied?"

"As I suspected." John set the cup onto the saucer and picked up his fork. "You're not a vampire."

"You won't laugh when my fangs pierce your jugular."

"Your fangs shan't come near my neck," John moved another flannel cake from the platter to his plate. "You haven't delivered my concerts."

"You haven't submitted the venues, my musical man." Kellen stuffed the last flannel cake into his mouth and then dabbed pear jam from his fingers onto the ivory tablecloth. "These are quite tasty. I may pick another year and return for seconds."

John set down his fork and studied Kellen. Just how far could this illusionist carry the game? To his satisfaction, Kellen, although still leering, squirmed under his stare.

"Steinway Hall," John said, holding the gaze. "The Metropolitan Opera House."

"And?"

"Castle Garden."

Kellen choked on his flannel cake. "That's impossible!"

John picked up his fork. "Then no deal."

Kellen rose slightly, leaned across the table, pried cold fingers into John's cheeks, and pulled him close.

"O ye as yet undervalued protégé of Maestro Seymour Cassidy, music mogul of nineteenth century Europe, now manifested in you." Kellen's black eyes sparked with dark excitement. "Be prepared to finally, finally accept your due."

The glass panes violently rattled; the shade snapped to the top. John dashed to the window just as a large crow flew into the torrents. He pulled the blind back to its halfway mark and then turned to the table. No Kellen.

However, the remnants of breakfast remained, along with Mama Prudie's dishes and tablecloth. So Kellen had chosen a distracting moment to slip out, very clever. Before John could process that fact or the disturbing events of the last hour, he heard a faint tapping on the door.

"Who is it?" John called out.

"Telegram, sir!" a childish voice replied.

John unbolted and unlocked the door, then paused, as his stomach took a sickening plunge. He hadn't yet figured out Kellen, but Kellen obviously hadn't departed this way.

He flung open the door.

A street urchin, about six, stood before him, holding out the telegram with his dirty little hand. John ripped the envelope open and read:

COME TO STORE OFFICE ABOUT POSSIBLE CONCERT - STOP - WILLIAM STEINWAY

John's heart nearly stopped at those words. Was this a trick? A trance? Was he now insane, like Granny Spencer and his mother? Or could Kellen Wechsler, odd and sly, really be musically connected?

The boy stood, outstretched hand quivering.

"Sir?" he asked between trembling blue lips and eyes filled with tears.

"I have no mon..." John began, then removed his wallet. Two dollars remained. He gave the boy one. The urchin's face lit up like tree candles on Christmas day.

"Thankee, sir!" The boy sped off.

"Hold on!"

Nothing but the clomping of the boy's shoes on the stairs. John ran down the hall after him.

"Tell Mr. Steinway I will be there before noon."

"Yes, sir!" the boy shouted back.

John flew into his best and cleanest clothes, hands fumbling at buttoning, zipping, and tying, heart pounding. If the telegram was a prank, John would look like a fool. If he was hypnotized, ought he not awaken by now? But if the telegram was authentic...

He guzzled the last of the coffee, then raced out of the garret and down the stairs, ignoring the derelicts sleeping it off and frantically hailing the first cab.

"Where to?" the driver asked.

"Fourteenth Street," John panted as he stepped inside. "Steinway Hall."

During the ride from one end of Manhattan to the other, John tried concentrating on street scenes as the cab passed them, but he kept thinking of his destination, home to the notorious New York Philharmonic Orchestra, scene of the sold-out concert of Russian virtuoso pianist Anton Rubinstein, and the setting where Charles Dickens had read from his works.

Before long, the cab stopped in front of the four-story stone building, stately with its front pillars and tall arched windows, as it dwarfed the other buildings in that block. John paid the driver and stood outside, contemplating the magnificent threshold he would soon cross. The building reputedly contained seven hundred of the finest gas lights, as well as one hundred award-winning pianos for sale. Stepping inside could irrevocably change his life's course. John straightened his shoulders and opened the door.

He had no sooner walked into the showroom when a thin man, gray-haired and clean-shaven, bony hands clasped in a desperate plea for a sale, hastened to greet him.

"Sir, may I help you?" The desperation in the salesman's expression turned to despair as he eyed John's shabby suit.

"I'm here to see Mr. Steinway."

"Mr. Steinway is a very busy man. Perhaps an associate can assist you."

John held up the telegram. The salesman put on his spectacles and read it, skepticism at John's words becoming open disbelief.

"Wait here," The man refolded his spectacles and tucked them into his pocket.

"Thank you."

The salesman scurried away to a second man, short with massive belly dangling over his belt, and whispered something to him. The second man sharply drew back in astonishment, which made his middle jiggle, and glanced at John, smothering his laugh with a quick cough into his handkerchief before traipsing from the room. The salesman returned to John.

"Mr. Murdoch is looking into the matter," he said.

"Thank you."

The salesman scurried away to a more likely customer. Mr. Murdoch did not return. Restless and wondering if the telegram might be a hoax, John wandered the showroom and noted beautiful rosewood square grands, a variety of uprights, and one magnificent grand with an ebony finish advertised as a "Steinway A."

"Mr. Simons," a voice said from behind him.

John turned around. It was Mr. Murdoch, much subdued, belly still quivering.

"Mr. Steinway will now see you."

"Thank you."

John followed Murdoch out of the showroom and down the hall until they reached the last door, a spacious office of dark glossy wood and closed heavy draperies. Framed awards covered the walls.

Grand Gold Medal of Honor
1867 Paris Exhibition

FIRST PRIZE MEDAL
AT THE
GREAT INTERNATIONAL EXHIBITION
In London, 1862
For powerful, clear, brilliant and sympathetic tone, with excellence of workmanship, as shown in Grand and Square Piano.

"Mr. Steinway will meet you momentarily," Murdoch said.

"Thank you."

A large banner hung behind Steinway's desk: *One concert on Saturday night, sells pianos on Monday morning.* On the deck lay a copy of Henry's story from last year. Before John could grasp the wonderful thing happening to him, the door opened, closed, and a man with a quick, even stride approached him and John thought "rain," for this man had neatly combed gray hair on a receding hairline, a gray and groomed beard; serious gray eyes behind small egg-shaped silver spectacles, one thick line of eyebrow across his forehead; and a gray pin-striped suit.

His smile, however, was open and sunny.

"Mr. John Simons?" The man reached out and grasped John's hand.

"Mr. William Steinway?"

"The very same." Steinway gestured to an oversized chair in front of his desk. "Please, take a seat."

Too bewildered for words, John sat.

"Mr. Simons, we're busy men, so I'll be brief. I have a large concert scheduled in my hall for June 16, featuring accomplished musicians demonstrating our latest models. They are expected to perform a mixture of solo original works and existing pieces. A one-hundred-piece orchestra will accompany them. I am, unfortunately, shy one pianist. Would you be interested?"

"Well...I..."

"The pay is small, a thousand dollars, but I can add another couple hundred for the short notification."

"I accept!"

"Well, then, I'll have Mr. Murdoch present the paperwork and explain the procedure and practice schedule. I won't be attending the concert, as I'm leaving for Europe this week, so Henry Ziegler, one of my trustees, as well as a beloved nephew, will be your person of contact."

"Thank you for the opportunity, sir."

"Thank you for relieving me of this dilemma," Steinway rose and again shook John's hand as Murdoch entered with the contract. In a daze, John listened to Mr. Murdoch explain the terms.

"Half now, half following the concert," Murdoch said, handing John a roll of bank notes after John signed the contract. "Do you have any questions?"

"Just one. Does Mr. Steinway do business with a Mr. Wechsler?"

"Wechsler?"

"Kellen Wechsler."

"Wechsler." Murdoch frowned as he considered it. "No, I can't say he does."

"You're certain?"

"Yes, I'd remember such an unusual name."

"Of course," John said, rising. "I must be mistaken."

John rode to M. Harrington & Sons, cashed the bank notes, and then called upon his father's tailor and ordered a new set of tails. The rest of the money, John decided as he placed it in his wallet, he would eke out for food. No need to pay the rent. No one had seen Cremmins in days.

As the cab rumbled back to the music hall, John pondered the morning's meeting. The telegram and the remaining cash were physical manifestations of his sanity. Mr. Murdoch confirmed John's suspicions. Kellen was a lunatic. Period.

But the breakfast remains on Mama Prudie's dishes were real, as real as the mice feasting on the crumbs. With a roar, John grabbed the broom and swung; the intruders abandoned their feast and squeaked to safety. Fine, Kellen was real, John thought as he stacked the dishes and carried them to the sink, but the so-called vampire could not claim this win. The credit belonged to Henry and his story. He must properly thank Henry, if he ever again encountered the dandy. In the meantime, he'd continue practicing on the empty music hall's stage. *The magic is in the melody.* Every selection must be perfect. Vigorously, John began pumping water.

Six weeks later, John stood in the wings of Steinway Hall, much as he once had at Hewes Music Hall, except he had Henry Ziegler and not Jackson for a companion. The auditorium held a vast universe of music-lovers, their faces blurred into a single unrecognizable mass. They filled the floor, the boxes, and even the doorways, for the sold-out concert had continued to entice patrons through the door, and Mr. Ziegler had insisted the box office keep the tickets moving.

"Nervous?" Mr. Ziegler asked, as he again peered around the curtain to gauge the audience reaction.

An interesting question, John decided, from a man who hesitated before smiling. A fat mustache didn't hide the lips pursed in thought; round glasses revealed anxiety in his eyes.

"No."

"Good."

A hush spread over the crowd as the emcee took the microphone.

"Ladies and gentlemen, I'd like to announce..."

"This is it," Mr. Ziegler pushed John forward.

"...Mr. John Simons!"

The clamor, as John crossed the never-ending stage, resounded in his ears and flowed through his veins to his fingertips, where they burned and tingled for release. The applause clattered away to silence as John settled himself at the Steinway grand. He paused, relishing the silence of three thousand barely breathing men and women. Then his hands struck the keys, a joyful waltz broke forth, and the applause exploded.

Far too soon, John exited, still reveling in the clapping following him offstage, unabashed admiration from New York's finest, for him, for his music. He had but one thought: how many of his father's colleagues attended?

Backstage, the air buzzed with excitement from investors and trustees alike, confident of a nice spike in sales come Monday.

"Have you heard?" a voice in the background piped up. "The great Timoteo Pasini is dead!"

"The composer for Giuseppe Garibaldi's funeral march?"

"Yes, the same!"

"But he's only 59!"

"Last Wednesday. It seems he..."

In the wings waited a man resembling his father in height and breadth, except he, with his clipped gray hair and a white and gray beard, broke out into a friendly smile and extended a warm hand.

"Phenomenal performance, Mr. Simons," the man said.

"Thank you," John replied, accepting the hand and wondering what it meant. "And you are?"

"James Roosevelt, vice president of the Chemical Bank of New York and one of the founding members of the Metropolitan Opera House."

Metropolitan Opera House? *Metropolitan Opera House?*

"I know my request doesn't allow sufficient lead time, but, Mr. Simons, would you consider performing at the house one week from tonight?"

"I...I..."

"The great conductor and composer Timoteo Pasini was to play selections from his operas in a rare piano performance, but he won't make it now, I'm afraid."

"Yes, I heard."

"I haven't spoken to the others, but I feel you'd make a fine replacement for the show. Would you be interested?"

"Yes, of course," John shook Roosevelt's hand again, this time with enthusiasm.

"Very well," Roosevelt said. "Come 'round to my bank Monday morning, and we can discuss terms."

Spellbound, John rode back to the music hall, reflecting on the magnificent concert of which he'd played a significant role, and the spectacular doors opening to him.

But if Kellen had his fangs in any of those circumstances, he wasn't forthcoming in admitting it. For just as mysteriously as Kellen had appeared, he had just as mysteriously disappeared. Now that his body and mind were again strengthened by proper nutrition, John realized his good fortune was his just reward to years of persistent hard work, thrust into public notice by Henry's generous review.

However, to be certain, John did ask Roosevelt at the contract signing if a certain Mr. Kellen Wechsler had contacted him. Roosevelt had looked confused at the question.

"Wechsler? Who is he?"

"No one important," John lowered his head and signed.

The entire concert seemed surreal and made the performance at Steinway Hall seem as insignificant as a Dana Hewes' event. The six-story building at 1411 Broadway Street was an entire block long and contained three tiers of private boxes. Except for selections from the operas *Imelda de' Lambertazzi* and *Giovanna Grey*, as a tribute to Timoteo Pasini, who ought to have occupied this center stage, every piece John played was his own creation. The audience expressed its enjoyment with a standing ovation, John's first.

Backstage beside a jubilant Roosevelt stood a man with a balding head, long curly beard of black sheep wool, eyes darting back and forth from Roosevelt to John, and facial expression bursting with the need to speak.

"Well done, John!" Roosevelt hugged John and thumped his back.

"Yes, indeed," his companion echoed. "I'm mightily impressed." He turned to Roosevelt. "Simons, you say?"

"Yes. John, meet Mr. Raymond Peabody. He's opening a restaurant on West 39th Street and has an unusual idea for publicity he'd like to discuss with you. Go ahead, Mr. Peabody."

"Well," Peabody said. "I'm giving a charity party on Independence Day."

Peabody paused, waiting for John's reaction.

"It's a good idea," John said cautiously.

"But not just any charity concert. Instead of raising money at the event, I'm hosting an elegant reception for the downtrodden. It would, of course, include appetizers from my restaurant, and piano entertainment by celebrated Mr. John Simons, if you so agree."

"And these people to whom you refer?"

"Immigrants coming into Castle Garden."

John's heart dropped.

"Castle...Garden?" John repeated. "Did you say, 'Castle Garden?'"

"Yes, Mr. Simons. What is the matter?" Peabody looked alarmed, and he steadied John with one hand and fanned him with his handkerchief. "Your face is ghostly pale."

Roosevelt was already hurrying back with a glass of water.

"Drink it," Roosevelt said. "You look as if you might faint."

"I don't want the responsibility of you fainting on the way home."

"I don't faint," John said with more vehemence than was necessary, causing the two men to exchange quizzical glances. But he accepted the water.

"Your color is returning." Roosevelt took the glass and handed it to a passing stage hand. "Must have been the excitement."

At that moment, one of the Vanderbilts appeared, and Roosevelt left to speak with him. This left John alone with Peabody.

"So what do you say, Mr. Simons?"

"I accept," John said.

"Good," Peabody handed him a card. "Come to my restaurant any day next week. I'll treat you to the best steak this side of Delmonico's and explain my plan."

"I'll be there," John said. "By the way, do you know Kellen Wechsler?"

"Who?"

The next two weeks flew past. Soon, July 4 arrived, and John loitered outside the circular brick-red sandstone building, full of portholes and platforms, as fitting for the former fort for the United States Army, which later had become, by turns, a saloon, restaurant, and, most importantly, a concert hall where Jenny Lind had once performed, courtesy of P.T. Barnum, who had brought the Swedish nightingale to America and managed her tour, the reason John wanted to perform here.

John blinked. "You worked for P.T. Barnum's circus?"

"I was a bareback lady."

"A bareback lady."

"Yes, on an elephant." Savannah laughed, a full deep melodious laugh.

Vicious fingers ripped into his heart. John flinched, and Peabody looked at him.

"Nervous?" Peabody asked.

John watched the throngs shuffle inside. Their faces were scared, tired, hopeful, dazed.

"No."

"Good. Let's get you set up."

Inside, the immigrants were separated from their boxes, trunks, and satchels, the latter being dispatched to the baggage warehouse, Peabody said. The sole light in the building was the natural one, supplied through a glass dome. Dozens of uniformed men milled about the rotunda, some working the registry, others assuring immigrants in words and in gestures, for many of them did not understand English, that they may use the building as temporary shelter. Others removed any of the ill or infirm who had escaped the quarantine and transferred them to State Emigrant Hospital on Ward's Island. Railroad agents pushed through the crowds, selling tickets.

Single file, each immigrant, including the women and children, stated his name, birth date, age, occupation, and destination.

"Name?" one registrar asked as he scanned the ship's listing.

"Viktor Zhuravlev."

"Spell it."

The immigrant shrugged and shook his head.

As John passed them into the large dining hall lined with tables and to the Steinway brought in for this purpose, for Steinway & Sons co-sponsored the event, he glanced at the faces of his unusual audience. Some were aglow; others, slumped on benches, singularly and huddled together, looked lost or frightened.

"That's the marvelous thing about music," Peabody said as they reached the piano. Nearby, Peabody's staff was setting out blinding white linens on long tables and unpacking the dishes. "It's the universal language. Everyone will understand it."

For the next two hours, John sprinkled complex compositions with renditions of *The Liberty Song* and *The Star-Spangled Banner,* as the half-starving refugees ravaged the food tables. Eventually, John switched to songs Papa Everett used to play, and these resonated with the shabby audience more than his masterpieces. Ladies in rags and shawls gradually released their inhibitions long enough to persuade their weary husbands to dance in the aisles with them. Children skipped in circles and twirled to the beat.

As John set down the lid, Peabody walked up.

"What a phenomenal success, I tell you! I even hired a couple of the...um...guests. I can't thank you enough."

"My pleasure."

"Say, I know you can't play without pay all the time, but would you consent to one last special request? Nothing as fancy or long as today."

"What are you suggesting?"

"I belong to old St. Patrick's. It has the most beautiful Erben pipe organ. I think the old cathedral sometimes gets forgotten, now that the

148

archdiocese has a new seat. What would you say about playing High Mass, just one time? I could arrange it through our priest."

"I'll play Sunday."

Peabody blinked, taken aback. "I didn't expect immediately. Certainly, you may ponder the request."

"On the contrary, I'm looking forward to fulfilling your wishes, and quickly."

"Well, thank you. Not trying to offend, but you don't strike me as the pious type."

"I'm not offended. And you'd be surprised."

The next day, John had an invitation for a special July fourteenth appearance at the Academy of Music, a four thousand seat opera house of New York's old money, eclipsed in popularity when New York's new money opened the Metropolitan Opera House five years ago. John smiled when he read the telegram and handed the urchin ten dollars.

"Thankee, sir!" The boy tipped his hat and dashed away.

Not long now, John thought with satisfaction, not long at all. He patted his wallet and hoped each card therein felt his hand. His hour with destiny drew near. He was ready.

On Sunday, John climbed to the choir loft of that Federal-style edifice and took his seat at the organ, one of the earliest sources of music from John's long-ago childhood, and John's first experience at awe, for the organ had cost fifteen thousand dollars at the time of its purchase in eighteen sixty-eight. As the Latin hymns reverberated off the plaster walls, John's spirit soared higher than the ceilings, knowing his father was facing the gold-leaf screen behind the altar, standing as proud as the marble statues, and loathing every note.

On Monday, John rode to the Russell mansion, the one home on Fifth Avenue actually renting rooms. The music hall had been sold; the new owner had already changed the locks. He'd soon lose crawling through the garret window as an entrance option, and anyhow, John no longer needed the garret. He'd made enough money to last several frugal years, even if he didn't play another show. That was highly unlikely, as more were scheduled at Steinway's, and Chickering Hall in Boston had asked John to perform in early August.

On Tuesday, John again visited his father's tailor and ordered a full wardrobe of new clothes. On Wednesday, he turned down an invitation to play for a party at Marshall Harrington's home, and on Thursday John turned down the Rutherfords, wincing as he did so, for he truly liked Della.

On Friday, Mrs. Lovell, the Russells' housekeeper, interrupted an extended practice session with a, "Mr. Simons, you have a visitor."

John ceased playing. "A visitor? Who?"

"She says her name is Bryga Bednarczyk."

Such a long time, John thought, no one since Flossie. Furthermore, Bryga belonged to his father, which increased her desirability.

"Mrs. Lovell, send her in."

Bryga still looked as plump as a little bird, but her black eyes had a softness to them that made her sweetly vulnerable. She wasn't wearing her chambermaid's uniform, but a mauve walking dress and matching bonnet. Despite her servant status, John rose at her entrance, which made her blush.

"Do you remember me, Mr. Simons?" Bryga asked, almost shyly.

"Such faithful industry! How could I forget?"

John stepped away from the piano and strolled to Bryga, causing her to look down and away as he drew close. He picked up a gloved hand, and, still gazing at her, tenderly kissed it, and then held it fast.

"Miss Bednarczyk, to what do I owe your visit this afternoon?"

"I've missed you, Mr. Simons." Bryga met his eyes and then added more boldly, "I'm offering you the pleasure of my company."

Still holding her left hand, John lifted her right hand and kissed that one, too. Clasping both beneath his chin, John asked, "Do we have an understanding, Miss Bednarczyk?"

"Indeed, sir."

John led her to the door and looked left and right. He turned back and smiled.

"Then let's go."

Playing the Academy of Music on Saturday was an especial thrill, as many of the attendees had even spurned his father in the past. Their enthusiasm as he strutted off the stage sounded louder and longer than any of the previous concerts. As John basked in the applause, one of the stage hands approached him.

"If you're looking for your manager, he's in your dressing room," the man said.

"My who?"

"Your manager, sir."

Briskly, John strode to the back of the house and flung open the door. There was Kellen lounging in his chair, smoking a cigar and sipping a brandy.

"It's time," Kellen said, setting down both cigar and brandy.

John pointed to the door. "Get out."

"The piper," Kellen continued, pausing to play a pretend flute, "always, always, always gets paid."

"I'm not paying an unstable extortionist." John turned to leave. "But I will call the police. You belong at Wards Island Asylum."

150

Kellen snapped his fingers and leaned out the window.

"Step it up, my man!" Kellen shrieked, snapping his fingers. "I haven't all night!"

With a lurch and an upward jolt, the carriage tore through the streets. Kellen bounced and swayed, clapping, cackling, and grinning through the dusty haze like the Cheshire cat. Horrified at this turn in his surroundings, John could only sit and helplessly watch. The carriage sped on and on and on, rocking and threatening to top, hooves thundering across the roadway, John's heart matching those gallops beat for beat, as full realization of the bargain settled into his mind.

Once, John tried peeping around the curtain, but Kellen slapped his hand away.

"Uh, uh, uh," Kellen trilled, waving a warning finger before John's face. "Uh, uh, uh."

Still surging to the carriage, Kellen sang under his breath:

Little Tom TU-cker
Sings for his SUP-per.
What shall we give him?
A vein full of blood, mmmmmmmmmmmmmmmmmmm...

Abruptly, Kellen jabbed John's side, and the carriage skidded to a halt.

"We're heeeerre!" Kellen threw back his head and giggled. "We. Are. HERE!"

Kellen leaped to the ground. In seconds, he was flinging open John's door. With a low mocking bow and a swoop of his arm, Kellen boomed, "Maestro, come, forth!"

Slowly, John stepped down and gazed uncertainly at his surroundings. The only barrier between them and the cliff's edge was a large tower, which Kellen was now unlocking.

"You live here?" John asked, unsure of anything anymore.

"Well, you might say that," Kellen said. "And you might not. Either way, a bargain is a bargain."

With a fiendish grin, Kellen's hands, cold even through his gloves, firmly grasped John's neck. Up ahead, the door creaked open.

"You have drunk deeply of success," Kellen murmured, the tip of his frigid nose touching John's warm one. "Tonight, it is my turn to drink."

John swallowed against the pressure in his throat and the horror snaking up it.

"Deeply," Kellen added, grasping tighter. "So very deeply."

Grabbing John's hair at the scalp, Kellen pulled John up the steep stone staircase, with John tripping and stumbling all the winding way to the top, a small round room with one round window. Moonlight threw evil beams across the floor and over the room's lone piece of furniture, a red velvet armchair. His star had ducked behind a cloud.

"Sit," Kellen said.

He licked his lips, glistening wet in the moon's soft glow, and then smacked them hard. Without hesitation, John sat, closed his eyes, and waited for death...or worse.

I will take it, John told himself, regretting nothing, every applause worth it. Whatever happens, I will take it.

With an exhilarated squeal at John's submission, Kellen hopped from one foot to the other, rubbing his hands together and then prancing across the room and back, sliding onto John's lap to pat John's cheeks and swipe his nails down John's throat. He skipped widdershins around and around and around the chair. And still John sat, unmoving, waiting.

Abruptly, Kellen wound his arm about John's neck and played it like a piano with his other hand. Then Kellen wound a hair lock around his index finger and kissed it.

"Mine," Kellen breathed into John's ear. "Mine, mine, mine, mine, finally, all mine."

After a quick nip on an ear lobe and a few happy pants, Kellen's tongue slipped down, and farther down. It flickered here; it fluttered there, short, frantic licks, with Kellen grunting in frustration. Finally, with a happy guttural moan, Kellen sank his talons into John's chest. John flinched but held firm. He felt the graze of canines. Kellen's mouth was ice, and it was opening wide.

In full resignation, John closed his eyes. Whatever would be, would be.

www.ingramcontent.com/pod-product-compliance
Lightning Source LLC
Chambersburg PA
CBHW030347180626
46812CB00007B/2788